PAYBACK IS A MUTHA

PAYBACK IS A MUTHA

WAHIDA CLARK

KENSINGTON PUBLISHING CORP.

DAFINA BOOKS are published by

Kensington Publishing Corp.
850 Third Avenue
New York, NY 10022

ISBN 0-7394-6634-8

Printed in the United States of America

To my favorite uncle, John.
The world would be a much better place
if there were more men like you. RIP.
Your favorite niece, Wahida

Acknowledgments

All praise is forever due to the Creator. To my family and supporting cast, you all know who you are. Thank you for your continued support and dedication. I love each and every one of you.

To all of my fans, there would be no me without you. I love y'all and thank you so much for your loyalty and support.

To all of you authors out there trying to get published, stay focused and keep writing. This isn't a process that happens overnight.

Nikki Turner, I enjoy our visits, so as soon as you get your next breather come holla at your sister. My newest fam, Mark Anthony, you about as real as real can get. Don't change and thanks for all of the books you send me. Brenda Thomas, thanks for your letters and I can't wait for your next book. Relentless Aaron, the Granddaddy of this new writing hustle, thanks for your words of wisdom. Darren Coleman, I appreciate the books you send me as well. They are all page-turners.

To the other authors who send me books and shout-outs: K'wan, Carl Weber, A.J. Rivers, Mike Sanders, Marvin Ellison, Valencia Williams, Keisha Irvin, Darrin Lowery. I appreciate the love.

Project Pat, don't forget you told me you was gonna wear that FREE WAHIDA CLARK T-shirt on 106 and Park. Yup! I'm puttin' you on blast. Now the whole world is waitin' and watching. Glad you're out. Can't wait to hear what you puttin' down in the studio. Money Mike Reid! It's all about you, playboy. Let's get this money. My little brother, Chi-Ali, I think I done spoiled you enough! Get to writing! Latif Lamar and the entire Paper Chase fam, stay up. My big brother, Al Saadiq Banks, you wrong for gettin' ghost on your sis, but it's all good. Caught 'em Slippin' was tha bomb!

Acknowledgments

Renay Coachman, you are da bomb! You know I got mad love for you for helping me decide on a title after mine got jacked and for reading everything I throw at ya. Other helpers on this project, Kim Moffet, Bridget, Twin (Lampkin), Tee Tee, Robyn, Andrea Walker, Dee Malloy, Mesha Honeycutt, my roommate, Angelia A. for her help, Brenda Walker, and Happy, thanks for the Memphis Tour. Baby Agnew, Jennifer Branch, Keisha Bruton, K.K. Walls, Maria, Adrienne, Jan Livingston, Kareenah, Ebony, Karen, Phyllis Smith, Angela F., TuTu, may your son RIP. Keep writing that poetry, and my prison mom, Dianna Sanchez, keep ya head up, Lashawn James thanks for the pens and the good meals, my other hair stylists Yolanda Burgess and Karen Brown along with the rest of the Alderson crew.

Karen Thomas, editorial director at Kensington, I love the way you handle business and how you are always willing to listen to my feedback. Thanks Lydia Stein. Jeracha Estavez, you are the bomb diggity! Marc Gerald and Earl Cox, I appreciate the teeth you had to pull on my behalf. Keep doing what y'all do.

To all of the bookstores, street vendors and book clubs, especially Raw Sistaz and Just Between Girlfriends, thank you.

Oh, I can't forget my brotha and partna, Kwame Teague. Your mind is awesome. Shout-out to Victor Martin, Joe Black, Buddy Row, Trick Daddy, C-Murda, Ce Ce Greathouse, Kaywan, and Seth "Soul Man" Ferranti.

Last, but not least, to my loyal team: Fisepe " Ice" Vival, Mike Reid, Dempsey Nolan, Raphael Spencer, Ronald Thompson, Eric Van Buren, Stanley Bellamy, Tennette "Missey" Jackson, Steven Dixon, Aaron Bebo, William Ewing, Andre Garfield, Tysheem Crocker, Dontez Mack, Doggy Mac that Philly Cat, Intelligent Tareef Allah, Parish Sherman, Bonta, Jessie Leflore, Shawn "Jihad" Trump.

Jules Rutledge of *Felon* magazine, thanks for the interview.

Acknowledgments

I know I forgot some people. My original acknowledgments got lost, so I'm coming off the top. If I forgot you, forgive me and I got you on the next go-round.

Holla at ya girl!

Wahida Clark
P.O. Box 8520
Newark, NJ 07018

Wahida Clark@hotmail.com

1

SHAN AND BRIANNA

"Gurrll, guess what?" Shan was almost jumping up and down as she shouted at her best friend Brianna through the phone.

"Why are you screaming?" Brianna asked with obvious agitation.

"I got the job, girl! I got the J-mutha fuckin' O-B!"

"Which one? You done interviewed with damn near fifty thousand people."

"The computer instructor for the prison, FCI Memphis. They just hung up."

Brianna sucked her teeth and rolled her eyes. "It took them long enough. I would have changed my mind. I don't see why you want to work for the prison system or work, period! All these niggas out here with money."

"Bitch, please! Everybody ain't a gold diggin' hoe like you. I need my own cash and I don't want to suck dicks to get it!"

"You better get with the program. What the fuck you think these niggas are for? There's absolutely no excuse for bitches like us to be broke!" Brianna shrieked in bewilderment. "And the last time I checked you were talking to two niggas! Where are they! You ditched them? Sometimes I don't understand your line of thinking." Then she frowned. "Working at a prison?"

"Bitch, just because you were in the BOP, and I choose to work for the BOP, don't hate. Congratulate! Plus, I've only been kickin' it with Calvin for a month. He likes me because he sees it ain't all about the cash with me. I'd rather get my own and have my own."

"Girlfriend, please! Do you hear yourself? Like I said, you better step up your game and get with the program. You can fall for that weak shit if you want. That nigga knows it's all about the cash. Niggas ain't nothin' but tricks."

"Do you, B, 'cause you know I'ma do me, so are you down to help me celebrate or what?"

"Like I said, if you were on top of your game—"

"Girl," Shan interrupted, "I bet you even hustle niggas in your sleep! Don't you?"

They both burst out laughing. Brianna knew for sure that Shan was telling the truth. "Let me make a few phone calls and I'll call you around nine. Dress to impress. You know I gotta kill two birds with one stone. I'ma celebrate with you and see who I can get with later." Brianna said.

"Yeah, I know how you do. But don't worry about me dressing to impress. You just make sure you are here by nine. Don't call at nine. Be here at nine! Peace out."

"Wait. What are you getting ready to do?" Brianna asked.

"Take a beauty nap. What you think?"

"Whatever, hoe. Do you."

"I'm trying. Peace."

After Brianna hung up the phone she dialed Yolanda, her hairdresser. "Landa, what's up? This is Brianna."

"I know who this is." She snapped. "What do you want? I have two bitches under the dryer, two at the sinks, the one in my chair and three waiting. You just came here two days ago, so no, I can't squeeze you in!" Yolanda rattled off.

Brianna sucked her teeth and rolled her eyes. "How do you know that's why I'm calling?"

Brianna was busted.

"Hoe, I know you, so stop playing games. I told you I'm busy."

"Too busy for an eight-pack on top of what I usually pay?" Yolanda was thinking. Her regular fee plus an eight ball of coke? "Yeah. That's what I thought." Brianna snapped back. "What's the best time to come?"

"Be here at two, Brianna. Not two fifteen, two thirty. And bring my shit!"

Brianna hung up without responding.

She stood in front of the mirror as she pinned up her $1,200 weave. "Where should we go tonight?" she asked the mirror. It was Friday night, and she wanted to take full advantage of it. Her girl, Shan, loved the hip-hop clubs, but B's first preference was anything where the *real* ballers hung, so she knew she had to choose the spot.

Her and Shan had been friends since the third grade. Everyone thought that they were family. Shan was closer to Brianna than her own blood sister. Unforeseen forces bound them closer together, like when Shan's parents were killed in that fatal car accident, and when Brianna got pregnant in the seventh grade and her mother put her out. They really leaned on one another. Even though Brianna lost the baby, her mother still wouldn't take her back. When social services came and took Shan and her brother, Peanut, away, Brianna was homeless. When a relative came and rescued them from the group home, that's when they took Brianna off the streets. Her mother didn't allow her back home until she went to the tenth grade.

Other than their copper complexions, they were night and day in just about every way. Brianna had those full pouty lips, while Shan had dainty sensuous ones. Brianna's nose was full; Shan's was a cute little button. Brianna's onion screamed, "Goddamn!" Shan's onion screamed, "Dayuum!" Brianna was tall and Shan was short. Brianna had to wear Gucci, Prada, and Chanel, while Shan preferred Sean John, Baby Phat, and FUBU. Brianna had the weave, fake nails, and boob job, while Shan had the locks, sported her real nails and refused to do the makeup thing. Brianna went to prison, while Shan now chose to work at a prison. Brianna lived large off the ballers, while Shan preferred the legit businessman or blue collar worker. Which is why everyone couldn't figure out how they remained so close over the years.

During Brianna's eighteen month prison bid the only three people who stuck by her was Shan, Peanut and one of her sugar daddys by the name of Nick. He kept money on her books and allowed her to run up his phone bill. She had mad love for Nick but she had been out now for almost a year and he felt like she still owed him. Brianna had recently told him that she gave him enough pussy to consider her debt paid in full.

Upon hearing the phone ring, Brianna snatched it up. "Hello."

"What up, B?"

"You."

"You don't even know who this is."

"Oh, I know who this is," she teased. "There is only one Shadee."

"Act like you know, girl! I thought I was gonna have to tap that ass. I need to swing by later on."

"Around what time? I got a hair appointment and me and my girl is going out. Can you come before six?"

"That'll work."

"Be on time, please."

"I got you."

She sucked her teeth. "Yeah, right." She hung up and immediately called Hook.

When Hook answered Brianna said, "Okay, nigga, I don't owe you nothing else. Your boy said he'll be here around six, which means eight. So handle yours."

"Handle mines?" he asked, sounding pissed off. "We straight as long as it's worth *my* while."

"Look nigga, that ain't got shit to do with me. I called you and it's on so now we are even. *Ya heard?*"

Hook didn't say anything for a minute. "Bitch, it's over when I say it's over! *Ya heard?*"

Brianna sighed as she slammed down the phone. "How in the fuck did I ever get involved with a sorry, punk ass nigga like that?" she said through clenched teeth.

Shadee didn't show up until a quarter after eight. When Brianna opened the door he grabbed her by her hair and gave her a big sloppy kiss. "What up, B?" he asked while squeezing her ass. His six foot two inch rich chocolate frame filled up the doorway. His white du rag was tied so tight it was making his already chinky eyes looked closed.

"I'm on my way out. My girl is waiting on me. When it comes to me you never have a concept of the time, do you?"

"Time is always on our side, B. And it's time to break me off a little sumthin' sumthin'." He grinned, causing that left dimple to wink.

"I don't think so. If you would have come a little earlier time would have been on your side. But, I'm dressed, ready to go and my girl is waiting on me."

"So, B, it's like that?"

"Right this minute? Yeah!" She tried to move his hands off her ass. "You always puttin' me on the back burner."

"Let me break you off, then," he whispered into her ear. "You can spare a few minutes for that, can't you?"

Brianna really didn't have to think that one over because Shadee could give tha bomb head. It felt like he had two tongues and like he put his nose in it.

"That got your attention, huh?" He laughed, sucked on her luscious lips some more, then picked her up and took her to the bedroom. "When are you gonna settle down for me?"

She slipped off her dress as soon as he put her down. "When can you settle down for me?" She flipped it.

"Why you gotta always answer my question with a question?" He slapped her on the ass.

"Oowww! Why'd you do that?" She rolled her eyes at him.

"Answer my question." He watched her nipples stick out as he played with them.

"That feels good." She slid back onto the bed, spread her thighs and ran her feet across his chest. "Can I answer you later?" She moaned as he licked the inside of her thighs.

"Yeah, I guess you can do that," he said as he spread her swollen pussy lips, smiled at the sight of her clit sticking straight out and sucked one of his favorite juicy pussies until he couldn't suck anymore.

As Brianna washed up, Shadee packed in a bag six kilos of powder, 8Gs, and he took two of those and threw them on the coffee table for Brianna. "Yo, B!" he called. Brianna's apartment was one of the spots he used as a stash spot.

As Hook and his boy Rob sat in the car waiting for Shadee and watching his Benz, Shadee was kissing B on the lips. "Can I come by later?"

"Call me, okay?"

"Give me another kiss." He leaned over and kissed her, then headed out the door.

"Here comes our boy." Rob was anxious as hell as he grabbed his pipe and they sprang from the car. As Shadee went to unlock the car door Rob smashed him over the head with the pipe, causing Shadee to let out a loud grunt as he fell over. Hook grabbed the black duffel bag, then him and Rob stuffed Shadee's limp body onto the backseat. Hook started the car and as soon as he got it out of park a forest green Hummer blocked him in and out jumped five of Shadee's boys.

2

SHAN

"Who is it?"

"Who you expecting?"

A smile lit up Shan's face as she opened the door for her brother Peanut and his boy Nick who used to be Brianna's sugar daddy. "I wasn't expecting you." She pushed up on her tippy toes and kissed him on the cheek. "So, to what do I owe the pleasure of this visit?"

"What you trying to say?" he asked as he walked in, inspecting her apartment with Nick right behind him.

"Boy, don't even try it. I ain't *trying* to say nothing—I said it! Why you walking through my house like you the social worker or somebody?" She teased him as she followed behind him. "Have a seat, Nick."

Even though he wouldn't say it, Peanut liked the gray and mauve color scheme she had going on throughout the entire apartment. But when you got to the bedroom it was full of black lacquer, red, yellow, light blue, and purple. It was weird. It was as if you had stepped into another apartment.

"What? You tryna hide something or somebody?" He closed her bedroom door.

"Not from you." She pushed him into the living room onto the sofa. She plopped down beside him. Peanut had been her mother, father, brother, and best friend since their parents were killed. Which caused them to have a very tight bond. "I don't know why you tryna front. Just say it. *'Baby sis, I just love your beautiful apartment. It's better and cleaner than what all my hoes got.'* "

Peanut just smiled at her and Nick burst out laughing. "Oh, so you got jokes? It's not better than mines."

"Yeah, right. But guess what?" She could barely contain herself.
"What?"

"I got the job and guess which one?" She was now off of the couch and hopping up and down.

"You making me dizzy. Sit your happy ass down."

"C'mon, Peanut. Guess which one?"

"I give up Shan, so tell me."

"You ain't no fun no more. The prison job. I got the computer instructor job I was telling you about." Shan plopped back down next to Peanut once she saw the look on his face.

"You know I don't want you working at a men's prison. What if a riot or something breaks out? You the police Sis. You ain't gonna get no special treatment," concern evident in his voice.

"Don't start." She jumped up again and headed out of the living room. "You know how much I wanted this one."

"Well, don't expect me to be happy for you. I don't feel right with my baby sister working around a bunch of crazy ass niggas, Shan." He heard the bedroom door slam. "Shan! Shan!"

"What?" She snatched the door open.

"Fix me something to eat."

"Fix it yourself! I'm getting ready to shower and get dressed. Me and Brianna will be going out tonight to celebrate; at least she's happy for me."

"Yeah, right! Brianna ain't never had no job; of course she's happy."

"Whatever!"

"What time y'all leaving and where are y'all going?"

Shan sucked her teeth. "I told her to be here at nine."

"Where y'all going?"

"You getting on my nerves now."

"Girl, you better tell me where you going," he warned as he stretched out onto the sofa.

"I don't know where we're going. It's her treat."

"Well, I suggest you find out."

"Nick, get your boy."

"Don't get me caught up in the middle of y'alls sibling rivalry." Nick wasn't getting involved.

"Oh, a'ight, then. I see how you do. When B comes let her in. I gotta go get ready."

"Shan, I'm serious; where y'all goin'?" Peanut pressed.

"I told you I don't know. Ask her when she comes." Shan kept it moving and left Peanut and Nick sitting in the living room.

"Yo, what's up, man? You know I don't need to be here when that bitch gets here. I'ma bust that thirsty bitch in her fuckin' mouth if I see her."

"Man, chill. I told you, you can't turn a hoe into a housewife. I'ma kick it here for a while. Go pick up that money from Darnell and come back."

Nick raised his six foot four inch frame up, gave Peanut a pound and headed for the door. "A'ight, man. I'll swing back by."

"Later." Peanut kicked back and grabbed the remote. He knew that Nick's pride was hurt. Brianna got all she wanted to get outta his man and dumped him. Peanut realized Nick was still sprung over her.

Brianna came out of her East Memphis town house and went in the opposite direction, missing the activity behind her. She jumped into her champagne colored Lexus and headed Orange mound to Shan's house.

Ten minutes later Brianna was knocking on the door.

"It's open," Peanut yelled.

Brianna stepped inside, smiled and licked her lips when she saw Peanut sitting on the couch. "Why is the door open?"

"Your boy Nick just left. You just missed him."

"Nigga, please." She put her Chanel bag down and stood directly in front of Peanut. "Where's your sister?"

"She's in the room getting dressed."

Brianna got down on her knees and began kissing Peanut as she unzipped his pants. "Did I ever tell you, you look like Michael Jackson when he was black and oh so fine?" She was planting kisses all around his neck. "Did I?"

"All the time," he said seductively. She kept kissing him, causing his body to heat up.

"A'ight now. You gonna get us busted. Shan can come out the room any minute now and your man said he'd be right back," Peanut said as he slid his hand up her dress.

"So what are you saying?" She began slurping on the head of his dick.

"You playing with fire, that's what I'm saying." He opened his legs wider and got in a better position. "Do you B, but make it quick." Peanut hit the mute button so that he could hear Shan, Nick, and the slurping sounds she made on his dick. "Damn . . . girl. Sssssshit . . ." He grabbed the back of her head. "Whoaa, girl, why you stop?" His dick was hard as ten bricks and was sticking straight out.

"You got a condom?"

"C'mon, B." He grabbed her head. "What you need a condom for? You was almost done!"

"I want some dick, nigga."

"Girl, stop playing." His dick was throbbing so hard that he was ready to grab it and finish his self off.

She sucked her teeth, got up and pulled a condom out of her Chanel bag. She ripped it open with her teeth and began putting it on a pissed-off Peanut.

"How you know I wanna fuck?" He watched her roll it down seductively on his dick with skill. "How bout I just want my dick sucked."

Brianna turned around, pulled her dress up above her waist,

bent over, grabbed onto the coffee table and spread her legs. "Daddy, don't do me like this. C'mon, please," she purred.

Peanut stood up and rammed his dick in Brianna's hot wet pussy. They both moaned out loud at the same time. Peanut thought his dick was going to explode. "Oh, shit, Daddy! That's right! Give me that dick!"

"Keep it down, B." Peanut was ramming her so hard his balls were making slapping sounds. "Aaah, bitch!" He went to cumming and so did Brianna.

All you could hear was heavy breathing. Then Peanut's limp dick slid out, the condom barely hanging on. He methodically snatched it off, pulled up his pants, and fell back onto the couch. Just as Brianna stood up and pulled down her dress, Shan's bedroom door came open. Peanut hit the mute button on the TV and began flicking channels while Brianna made a beeline for the bathroom.

"How long you been here?" Shan prodded.

"A couple of minutes, girl; hold that thought." Brianna hurriedly closed the bathroom door.

"You still here?" Shan stuck her nose up at her brother. "What's that smell? You need to put your boots back on." She grabbed a can of air freshener and began spraying it throughout the rooms.

"Do you have to overdo it?" Peanut was trying not to cough.

Shan looked at her brother as if he was crazy. "I think you forgot whose house you're in. It's time for you to go."

Knock, knock.

"Make yourself useful and get the door."

"It's your house, remember? You get the door," he teased. When she went to open it Peanut yelled, "It's open." And in stepped Nick. He always wore black. Black sweat suits, black jackets, black gators, black suits. The black contrasted uniquely against his high yellow skin. He favored the reggae artist Sean Paul.

Shan sucked her teeth and rolled her eyes at him. "What I do?" Nick asked.

"Brought my brother over here."

"I didn't bring him, he brought me." Nick casually said before turning to watch Brianna step out of the bathroom.

"You ready girl?" She headed towards Shan's bedroom to avoid Nick. He was too grounded and laid back for Brianna's taste. Deep down she knew that he was good for her. He was exactly what she needed but she wasn't ready for him; not at this point in her life when she was enjoying this climactic lifestyle.

Shan followed behind her. "Close the door," Brianna said with attitude. "What is he doing here?" Her arms were folded across her chest.

"I don't know. He came with Peanut." Shan shrugged it off. "How do I look?" She spun around in her all white tight leather Sean John shorts with the matching long sleeve jacket. "You like?"

"Girl, you almost look as good as me."

"Go 'head with that. Give props where props is due." Shan grabbed her leather Coach purse.

Brianna laughed. "A'ight, you got that. Those thigh high boots are bangin'! All you need now is a whip," she teased.

"Stop playin' and let's roll; I'm ready to get my party on."

"Me, too. If I can just get past the big, bad monster out there." B was referring to Nick.

"Girl, don't start with him. Let's just go." Shan turned off the bedroom light and led the way out. "Peanut, I'm out. Make sure you lock up."

Before Brianna could get to the door, Nick was up in her face. "Who the fuck you think I am?" Brianna tried to walk around him but he grabbed her arm.

"Peanut, get your boy." She tried to snatch away.

"Nick." Peanut had jumped up off the couch. "C'mon, man."

"Let me go, Nick. You're hurting me," Brianna warned.

"C'mon, man. Don't start this shit in my crib."

"Nut, let me holla at this bitch. Back up off of me man."

"Take this shit outside." Peanut was trying to free Brianna's arm from Nick's grip.

"We ain't taking nothing outside. I don't have shit to say to the nigga, so why is he harassing me?" When she snatched away from him he hauled off to punch her in the face but Peanut blocked the blow and pushed him towards the front door. Shan opened it up and grabbed his arm.

"Nick, I know you ain't swing at her in my house!" She was pulling him out into the hallway.

"I'm not even gonna let that nigga get me excited and ruin my evening. Punk!" Brianna yelled at him as the front door closed.

"You ain't right, B! You know that, don't you? I want you to chill out!" Peanut told her.

"I'm chilled; you need to be tellin' your boy that."

"I'ma get with him. Where are y'all going tonight?"

"That new club out on the East Memphis called The Premiere; you coming through? When am I going to see you again?" Brianna was like, *later for Nick; I'm tryna get with you again.*

"You can see me right now." Peanut leaned over and gave her a kiss.

"Stop playing Peanut, I'm serious."

"I'm serious, too. I can hit it right quick."

"You gonna get us busted."

"You wasn't saying that earlier."

"C'mon Brianna." Shan burst in the door. "He's in the car." She looked from her brother to Brianna. "You okay?"

"I'm fine."

"What time you coming home?" Peanut asked Shan.

"I'm grown. I'll be here when I get here. Now come on B. Lock the door Peanut."

They drove in silence as the Lex pumped the music of Ashanti, Vivian Greene, and Heather Hadley.

"Yo, you know you did Nick wrong, right?"

"Girl, fuck these niggas! I'll be glad when you wake the fuck up," Brianna spat.

"I'm just saying, B, you reap what you sow. That nigga held you down the whole time you was on lock. Then when he got knocked, you ain't give the nigga that same love back. But when he got out and came back up, you got back in—"

"Until I got tired of him and now it's a wrap." Brianna cut Shan off and finished off her sentence. "So what? Shit, he'll get over it. I'm sure this ain't the first time he got used for the trick that he is."

"I don't know what to say about you." Shan shrugged in disgust.

"Whatever, hoe. Now tell me about this Calvin."

"Hold up; guess who had the audacity to call me last night?" Shan asked.

"Who? And don't think I'm letting you get away with not telling me about Calvin."

"Girl, shut up and guess who had the nerve to call?"

"Derrick," Brianna guessed.

"Nope," Shan teased.

"Jay."

"Nope."

"Girl, who?" Brianna was losing patience.

"Kris," Shan finally told her.

"Aw, hell naw! Did you talk to him or hang up on his ass? I hope you called the police and told them. Ain't that violating his restraining order? You should have let Peanut kill his ass when he wanted to. I hate the way he would bruise you up. You didn't talk to him, did you?"

"No. I hung up. Shit, I should have killed him myself. Police officer or not," Shan reminisced.

"Hell yeah. What did he say?"

"I hung up. I didn't even want to hear it."

"That's what I'm talkin' bout," Brianna encouraged Shan. "But fuck him! I wanna hear about Calvin. Why is he such a big secret? Is he that fine? Don't worry, you're my girl; I won't take him from you!"

If Shan only knew. Brianna's grimy ass fucked Kris on several occasions resulting in a pregnancy that she aborted.

"Bitch, pleeze! He is very fine but he is not your type. Meaning, he's not a baller or a trick. He's a businessman."

"What kind of business?" Brianna inquired.

"I met him when I went to get my brakes fixed. He owns an auto repair shop on the South Memphis."

"I hear you. So why haven't I met him?"

"Girl, please, I haven't heard back from him," Shan was embarrassed to say.

"What do you mean? Why not?" Brianna had this huge frown on her face.

"That's a whole 'nother story!"

"What happened? What happened, hoe?" Brianna prodded.

"I don't want to talk about him."

"C'mon, Shan. Tell me." The suspense was now more than Brianna could stand.

Getting agitated, Shan spat, "We fucked and I haven't heard from him since! A'ight?"

"What? No shit? That ain't our style, Shan. How'd you let him play you like that? Please tell me you got a couple of grand outta the nigga! I know I taught you better than that!" Brianna said with much attitude.

"Girl, please. You the last person I'll let teach me anything."

"So what happened? Did you or didn't you get some paper?" Brianna was talking to Shan as if she was a moron.

"No, I wasn't tryna hustle the nigga for no dollars but we'd been vibin' off one another, and he made plans to take me to Las Vegas the weekend of my birthday. I told you that."

"Damn, that reminds me. We haven't kicked it since your birthday?"

"No, we haven't. You've been doing what you do best, hoeing around, hustlin' niggas, and I've been doing what I do, working and job hunting."

"I'ma act like you didn't say that. But for the record, don't hate the player, hate the game. Now, finish telling me about Las Vegas.

And please tell me you at least milked Las Vegas until it couldn't be milked anymore."

"Brianna do you ever rest from getting your hustle on?"

"No, I don't. And you's a sad bitch, if you tell me you didn't milk that nigga."

Shan waved her hand at her. "Anyways, Vegas was all good. We had a ball." Shan's face lit up as she spoke. "We gambled and I won $4,700 and lost it all but about $600. We clubbed, we wined and dined and saw two old school shows, the Whispers and the Temptations. I really had a good time. That was almost a month ago. I haven't heard from his ass since. The nigga won't even return my page." Shan looked over at Brianna and said, "B, I know my pussy is worth a damn return phone call!"

"Girl fuck him! Don't let no sorry ass, ungrateful nigga get you down. Tricks that can take you to Las Vegas come a dime a dozen."

"It wasn't all about the trip. It was the vibin' and the dick!" Shan had to smile at her rhyme.

"Oh, shit! Don't say the nigga had it goin' on with the dick?"

"I won't say it then." Shan pursed her lips.

Brianna was staring at Shan with her mouth open. "No. How good was it? Tell me."

Shan laughed. "I promise you. You ain't never came the way I came."

Brianna's mouth was wide open. "Dayum, girlfriend. That dick must have been tha bomb!"

"It was girl, I put that on my mama. Aw, shit, look at all these niggas out here." Shan was checking out the club and all the black folks that were out to enjoy the evening.

I hope you find us a parking spot close by. We don't need to be walking for miles and miles."

"Shit. You know I'm not parking my Lex on the street. This is a night for valet parking. You know my rules."

"Whatever hoe! Just get me in the club so that I can celebrate."

"They shook, shook, shook/ah made you look/you a slave to a page in my rhyme book." Shan was feelin' Nas as his beats was

pumping her up. They squeezed their way right on over to the bar. Brianna was already scheming on how to get seated in the VIP section.

"So far so good." Brianna stated her approval of the high-tech décor and atmosphere of the club. "Crowded but cool. Black folks love a nice spot to go and chill out." Then she nudged Shan. "Shan, look at that shoddy hoe. I know the fashion police must be nearby."

"B, don't start," Shan warned before turning to see who Brianna was cracking on. "Oh, hell no!"

"See. I didn't even have to tell you who I was talking about."

"What do she have on?" Shan was puzzled. "Looks like a night-gown over a pair of biker shorts and some cowboy boots. Something has to be wrong with her. How did she even get in? I thought this place had a damn dress code the way ole boy was looking us up and down at the door."

"Queen, please. You know what time it is. We got the look be-cause of how good we look!" Brianna bragged as they both sang. "Okay!"

"Uh-oh. Here come the drinks." Brianna's night was now falling into place.

"Brianna, you know how I roll. I gots to see my drink getting poured," Shan, being the responsible one, said. "You can't trust these niggas. Now let's get that table over there." She pointed be-hind them. Shan eased off of the stool and grabbed Brianna's hand. Brianna grabbed her drink and winked at the older brother who sent them over, ignoring Shan's warning. Before he got off his seat to come to where she was, her and Shan were already lost in the crowd.

"Bitch, don't make me spill this!" Brianna yelled over the music.

As soon as they found a table and sat down Sean Paul was telling somebody to, *"Gimme the Light and Pass the Dro."* Shan said "Yeah! I'll be back, B!" and went to get her dance on.

Brianna sipped on her drink as she scanned the room. Her eyes landed on this baller named Skye. He wore a baby face but the neatly trimmed goatee added some maturity. His cheekbones were high, making him look Indian. He wasn't all that cute but she heard that his pockets made up for it. He was six foot three, light brown and had light green eyes. His hair was cut to a low fade. He had on a tan Enyce velour sweat suit and had two hoochies grinning all up in his face. She had heard about Skye and they had crossed paths a few times but she'd never had the opportunity to talk to him. She kept staring at him until he looked over at her.

"Come here," she mouthed. He smiled and looked back and forth between the two honeys before him and looked back at her. "Fuck them hoes! Come here!" she mouthed again. She never took her eyes off him as he said something to the two hoochies and made his way over to her table.

"Damn playboy, is it really that serious?" B asked as she looked him up and down.

He grinned and she was liking the smile and the gorgeous set of teeth. "That depends on you." He was checking her out as well.

"All I want is a number."

"You called me all the way over here just for a number?" He teased as he pulled his chair closer to hers.

"I gotta start somewhere. What else do you want me to ask for?" she flirted.

As he pulled out a business card two of his boys came over. "Yo Skye, let me holla at you."

He nodded to his boy and then passed B his card. "What else do you want?"

"I want you to ask me my name."

He flashed them pearly whites again, and stood up. "I'll get at you before the night is out."

"Damn, he looks paid." Shan whispered teasingly in Brianna's ear as they watched him walk away. "Who was that? You just met him?" she said as she sat down. "Do you already know him? Damn, you move fast."

"His name is Skye and I plan on getting to know him before we leave up out of here." She put his card in her purse. "So you're through getting your dance on?"

"For now, yeah." Shan was fanning herself and looking around for a waitress. "I'm thirsty as hell! Oh shit, this is my song!" She snapped her fingers and began chair dancing while singing along with Khia. *"All you ladies pop that thang like this/shake your body don't stop don't quit/just do it, do it, do it, do it, do it now."* She abruptly stopped and began frowning.

"What's the matter with you?"

Brianna turned towards the door to see what or who had Shan's thong crawling up the crack of her ass. Who she saw was a nigga who she wanted to see but at the same time didn't want to see if that was who her girl was sweatin'. It was Briggen. One of the biggest ballers in Memphis. Foine. Six foot two, clean shaven and cut up. Nigga looking good as Tyson Beckford. He was dressed in all black and he was busy meetin' and greetin'. His demeanor reminded her of the character Nino Brown in *New Jack City.* A little more polished but very cocky. Hook had promised to introduce her to him but he never did. Shan snapped her out of her thoughts.

"I'm ready to go," she snapped.

"What's up?" B asked while deep down she was filled with envy and hoping that Briggen wasn't the one who took Shan to Las Vegas.

"There goes that nigga Calvin I was telling you about."

"Damn, Shan, you should know who you're opening your legs for!" She shook her head back and forth in disgust. "You call him Calvin. Who the fuck is Calvin? That's Briggen. He's one of the biggest dope dealers in Memphis. He also owns Sharia's Beauty Salon in the South Memphis, that auto shop you went to, a day-care center and nine times out of ten the way he stepped up in this place, he owns this club. For real, for real, if you play your hand right you got it made in tha shade; why you playin'! The only downside is he has at least three or four *steady* bitches who he fucks with."

Shan rolled her eyes at Brianna, not wanting to believe what she just heard, and sank deeper into her chair.

"Ain't this some shit!" she mumbled.

"Yeah, I must say so myself." Brianna said, not able to conceal her jealousy. "So what's your next move?" She was watching everybody who was somebody trying to holla at Briggen as he got closer to their table.

"I want to get the fuck outta here. My night is shot. I feel like I'm about to throw up." She stood up. "Let's bounce." When she went to turn around she ran right into a hard chest and some Armani cologne.

"I thought that was you."

"Do I know you? " She looked at him as if she was confused. "Oh! Your name is Calvin; or is it *Briggen*?"

3

FOREVER

"Thompson! Let's go! You're out of here!" The CO yelled as he kicked the bars.

Forever pulled the covers from over his head. He was just dreaming that he had Beyoncé's legs thrown over his shoulders and he was knee deep in that pussy.

"What'd you say? Who did you call?"

"You, Thompson! Let's go! You want out the hole or what? I always did think that you liked it over here," the short muscled CO yelled.

"I don't like your big mouth."

"What was that?"

"You heard me man." Forever stood his six foot frame up and stretched. If the rapper Method Man was to look at Forever he would be looking at himself. Even their raspy voices resembled. The only difference was the light brown eyes that Forever owned. "Damn," he muttered. "I was just getting ready to bust a nut inside Beyoncé." He stretched again, trying to make himself become fully awake. He had another night of uninterrupted sleep, being that his neighbor was dragged out two nights ago in a strait jacket. Every night he would scream, holler, and cuss at the imaginary children in his cell. So Forever was blessed with a few days and nights of peace and quiet all to himself. Seg will fuck with a nigga's mind. The only thing Forever liked was he had the cell all to himself. Being by yourself in a cell is a big blessing. The other advantages were you didn't have to work and your meals were brought to you. But from there, it was all downhill. Locked down twenty-three hours a day, one phone call a month, a shower every other day and your mail constantly fucked with. The only thing to do was read, sleep, write letters, and do push-ups and sit-ups. And in Forever's case, no visits. After he pissed off his hard-on he washed his face, brushed his teeth, and threw on his prison gear. He had been in the hole, or seg, for eight months.

The prison officials finally decided to end their eight-month-long investigation on him. An inmate overdosed on some heroin and Forever was the suspect only because the dead person was his cellmate and Forever was the number one suspect of getting drugs smuggled into the prison. However, they were never able to prove it. Surprisingly, no one was brave enough to come forward and rat him out.

He packed up all of his belongings and was now ready to go back to General Population. He missed not being able to get his hustle on. So, hell yeah, he was looking forward to going back into GP.

As soon as the officer opened the door, Forever picked up the plastic bag with his belongings and headed to the civilization that he knew eight months ago. As he walked through the halls many peeps were hollering at him. When he reached his unit his right-hand man and cousin, Zeke, was mopping the floor. Zeke looked like the stereotypical prison convict. He had dark skin, a bald head, was five foot eleven, two hundred sixty pounds, with plenty of tattoos hugging his overly muscled frame. He had a thin scar running from the back of his ear down to his shoulder blade. The flip side is he looked good and had a charming personality that goes over well with the ladies.

"What up nigga?" Forever yelled.

Zeke looked up at his boy and grinned. "It's about time your punk ass came off of vacation."

"Man, I wish I was on a vacation." They gave each other dap and then embraced. "I'm glad as fuck to get outta there. Let me throw this bag in my house and jump on this phone. I gotta call Nyla. I haven't got any mail from her in over a week."

"Then what?"

"Then what? I'ma shit, shower, and shave. After that I'll get with you. I know you're ready to bring me up to speed on things but foreal, foreal, I'm in no hurry." He smiled. "I got that feeling that I won't like what I'm gonna hear."

"You're right about that. I'll be out in the yard." Zeke went back to mopping the hallway.

The first time Forever tried to reach Nyla, his wife and daughter's mother, he didn't get an answer. So he decided to go ahead and shower and shave. As soon as he did that he was called to get his property and to see his counselor for work placement. After he argued to no avail about losing his old job of cleaning the visiting hall he was assigned to a different orderly job for the new computer teacher. He would be cleaning her office, the computer classroom and hallway. After that he headed outside to the weight pile and was anxious to breathe some fresh air. As soon as he stepped foot outside he stopped, inhaled, looked up to the sky and welcomed the sun beaming down on his face. "Yeah!" he yelled out.

"What up Forever!" Jay yelled, disturbing Forever's moment. Forever's eyes scanned the yard, taking in the typical prison yard scene. Blacks in one area. Whites in another. Latinos over there. Also the typical red bandannas, blue bandannas, tattoos.

"Bout time nigga!" Moose strained as he lifted 270 pounds.

"Uh-oh! I know the drought is about to be over," Tone hollered.

Forever nodded at everybody and went over to his partna in crime who was on the pull-up bar. Forever got down and proceeded to do two hundred push-ups. They both worked out in silence. When they finished Zeke said, "Let's walk." As they circled the track Zeke asked, "How's the family?"

"I hope a'ight. I haven't caught up with her yet. So what's up? Why has it been so damn dry? Where's Rice?" Rice was one of the officers who smuggled in Forever's dope.

"They walked our number one man off on some fucking an inmate bullshit." Zeke answered nonchalantly.

"What?" Forever said, not sure if he was hearing right.

"Yeah. Rice was coming in wearing red panties under his uniform and shit. He was getting fucked by that punk named Juwan. They got busted in the infirmary. Red panties and all!"

"Damn." Forever shook his head in disbelief. "What about Carter and Scott?"

"When Carter saw that, he got scared as fuck and transferred to Atlanta. Scott is still around but he just made lieutenant so he's chillin' for now. I can't talk him into doing shit. And you know the visit situation really ain't worth our while. We need some fresh meat. The market is off the meter. I went up a little on the prices because ya know these niggas still gonna cop. But the little shit I get in now is a fuckin' joke. You gotta handle your business, and fast."

"What'd you do?" Forever listened intently.

"An ounce of weed is a "G" and an ounce of powder is double that. I told them that's all we'll be moving. Everybody's waitin'. It's on you now."

Forever nodded his head. "How's your family?" He asked Zeke.

"Man, don't get me started. That bitch won't even bring my boys to see me and always bitchin' about how much money she need." They walked in silence some more until Zeke blurted out, "I'm just tryna maintain but that hoe be havin' me stressin'."

"I hear you man. Some nigga gotta be all up in her head for her to be trippin' like that."

"Her head! Fuck that! All up in that pussy!" Zeke spat. Now he was really pissed.

Forever had no comment for that. He switched the subject and Zeke filled him in on the jailhouse drama for the next half hour. "A'ight man. I'ma go try this phone again." Forever jogged back to the building.

When he reached the phones there was a long line. "Damn," he mumbled under his breath and leaned up against the wall. He hadn't held his woman or his five-year-old daughter Tameerah in eight months. He had to admit and be thankful that he was one of the lucky brothas who had a woman on the outside who was riding with him. Finally, after twenty minutes a phone came open. He quickly dialed home hoping that his wife was there. After the fourth ring he heard his daughter's voice and started smiling. She had the nerve to press five.

"Hello," she said.

"Hey Tameerah, baby. How's Daddy's baby?"

"Mommee! It's Daddee!" she yelled. "Hi Daddee."

"Hey baby. You okay? How's school?"

"It's fine. We got a rabbit."

"A rabbit! At home?" Forever acted shocked.

"No." She laughed. "At school. His name is Fred."

"I see. You miss me?"

"Yup. Here comes Mommee."

"I love you baby." Forever smiled.

"I love you too." Tameerah passed the phone to her mother.

"Hey baby. How are you? I miss you." She squeezed the phone tight.

"I'm out the hole."

"Are you?" She gasped.

"Yeah. I came out earlier today. Can you come see me this weekend? I miss the shit outta y'all."

"Not as much as I miss you." Her voice cracked.

"Y'all a'ight?"

"Other than you not being here, we're fine."

"How about money-wise?"

"I'm working part time for an insurance agency."

"Working?" Forever was surprised.

"Our stash is getting low. I know you didn't think it was going to last forever."

"Who watches the baby?"

"She's in school and she's not a baby anymore, Forever. I take her and pick her up. I'm here when she leaves and here when she gets out. Plus, I'm doing my little balloon hobby, as you like to call it."

Forever was silent, mulling things over in his mind.

"Everything's working out fine," she tried to assure him. "You know I have to keep busy."

"How does she like school?"

"So far so good. Let's just hope it lasts. Do you miss me?" Nyla ran her hand across her breast.

"Baby, you know I do. You don't even have to ask that."

"I just like to hear you say it."

"I'll show you how much when I see you this weekend. I can't wait to see you."

"I can't wait to see you either. You been dreamin' about fuckin' me or that bitch Beyoncé?"

"Be who?"

"Nigga, don't play with me!" she joked. "I'ma step into your dreams and beat that bitch's ass and then I'ma beat yours!"

"You know I only dream about makin' love to you. You love me?"

"Always and forever."

4

SHADEE

"What the fuck is this fool doing?" Hook laid on the horn as the forest green Hummer blocked him in. "Move the fuck outta the way!" he yelled.

"Shit, Hook, this looks like the jackers are gettin' jacked!" Rob said as he cocked his glock. "Ain't this a bitch! We bout to get jacked! Fuck! I told you we should have brought some more bodies for this nigga." Rob's adrenaline was pumping. Just the two of them were supposed to rob Shadee.

No sooner than those words left his mouth the car was surrounded. "Shadee is lying in the backseat!" Doc screamed in disbelief. *Pop! Pop!* He fired. "These niggas is busted!" *Pop! Pop!* The gunfire rang and glass shattered everywhere. Doc was hit in the arm while Rob, sitting on the passenger side, was hit in the head, the bullet bursting his head wide open. Two bullets caught Hook in the shoulder as he screamed out in pain. Glass and blood was all over. The windows on the passenger and driver sides were gone. The front windshield was all cracked up.

Hook was yelling like a bitch. "Shut up, nigga!" Teraney punched Hook in the face. "Move the fuck over!" He pushed him. "Get from under the fuckin' wheel!" Teraney pushed Hook over and jumped in the driver's seat. He was sitting on top of Rob's dead body.

Hook figured that he could get away since he saw that they were occupied with Shadee. He reached in his sock and pulled out his little .22 and pressed it to Teraney's temple. "Let me out right now, or I'm taking this chump with me! Ossssh! Ahhhh!" Hook yelled as Teraney knocked the gun from his hand. Slim crushed a piece of glass into his cheek. He was still yelling as the blood gushed out.

"You dummy!" Teraney said as he shook his head in disgust. "What was you planning to do with that little shit?"

"Shadee still breathing y'all!" Doc yelled as he felt his pulse. "We gotta move from this spot. Pop the trunk! Get something and tie my arm, I gotta stop this bleeding." He was barking orders. In a matter of minutes they threw Rob's dead body in the trunk and put Shadee in the Hummer. Teraney, Slim, Hook, and Jo Jo rode in Shadee's Benz. Doc didn't want to go to the hospital because he had a friend who could attend to his bullet wound.

"We gotta get Sha to the hospital." Slim said.

"Naw, fuck the hospital. Get him to a street doctor," Doc ordered.

"He almost dead man. By the time we find the street doctor he'll be gone." Slim looked at Teraney and Jo Jo for help.

"I'm with Raney. Fuck the hospital, we'll be taking a chance," Jo Jo added.

"We taking a chance either way. It's best to be safe instead of sorry. Fuck that. Let's get him to a hospital!"

"Hell, naw! He ain't going to no hospital," Doc yelled.

"We wasting time and you hurt. Let's do something instead of arguing like a bunch of bitches," Teraney said as he had made up his mind that his boy was going to see some real doctors.

When Shadee woke up he was looking up at bright hospital lights, lying in a bed at the "Med;" the local hospital. He now had fourteen stitches traveling down the back of his head. He tried to sit up but felt dizzy and his head was throbbing so he slowly laid back down. He felt around for a switch, button, or something to

"Naw. I wanna see Hook." Shadee began looking for his cell phone.

"Here man." Kay-Gee handed it to him.

Shadee grabbed it and dialed Teraney. "Teraney, what's poppin'? I need you to hold up."

"Won't nothin' be poppin' in a minute. You know I don't like to sit on shit like this. But if you insist, I'll hold up. But y'all need to meet me at our chillin' spot, soon."

"Wait for me. What do it look like?"

"What it look like?" Teraney looked at the phone as if he was insulted. "It looks like one of your bitches! And I hope you know which one."

"I'll holla at you later." Shadee turned off his cell phone, leaned his head back on the headrest, and closed his eyes. "Let's swing to our chillin' spot."

When they got to their chillin' spot, which was Kay-Gee's grandfather's crib, they entered the back and went down into the basement. Teraney and Jo Jo had tied Hook up, and he was naked, stretched out onto two folding chairs with a sock stuffed in his mouth. Jo Jo had on a painter's jumpsuit and a pair of goggles.

"Why is he tied like that?" Shadee wanted to know.

Jo Jo pulled out a chain saw, grinned and said, "I'ma cut his body in half. I always wanted to do this shit man."

When Hook heard that, he was tryna scream as his eyes got big as saucers and he tried to squirm loose.

Shadee tried to hold his balance as he walked over to Hook and pulled the sock out of his mouth. Hook began yelling, "Don't let him do this, man! I can take y'all to Rob's stash right now. Please man, don't let him do this," he pleaded.

"Who put you on me?" Shadee asked through clenched teeth.

"I don't know man. I was with Rob," Hook pleaded.

"Wrong answer." Shadee stuffed the sock back into his mouth and nodded towards Jo Jo who pulled the chain to start the chain saw. Everybody stepped back in anticipation.

Hook began withering like crazy as he pissed on himself.

"Hold up. This nigga ready to talk. Turn it off." Shadee looked down at Hook, who was shaking his head up and down.

As soon as the sock was pulled out of his mouth he blurted out, "It was that bitch Brianna. It was Brianna man! She put us on you. I swear!"

Shadee was embarrassed as hell. *That fuckin' bitch!* He was talking to himself in disbelief. *Is that hoe that desperate for money? All that we've been through and that trick got the nerve to set me up. All I ever did was look out for her.* No one in the room was saying a word. From the look on Shadee's face they knew that now was not the time for "I told you so's." Snapping out of his silent rage he asked, "Where's that nigga Rob's stash house?"

Hook began singing like a canary. "At his mom's. In the hallway there's a small door inside the linen closet. It's yours man, just let me go."

"C'mon y'all. Slice that nigga up!" Shadee ordered.

5

SHAN

"Oh, now I can't touch you?" Briggen grabbed Shan and gave her a big bear hug. He whispered in her ear, "Why are you treating me like this? I swear I haven't been able to stop thinking about you."

"I don't know you. Who are you?" She was trying to squirm out from between his arms.

"You don't know me?" he asked, surprised. "I could have sworn I heard you calling my name when I was lickin' on this juicy pussy."

"Nigga, please! What is your name? Is it Briggen or is it Calvin? I should have at least known who it was that I was allowing to lick my pussy!"

"Why are you so pissed about a name? Damn girl. My name is Calvin. My nickname is Briggen. That's what my friends call me."

"What about the other women who you fuck? Who are you to them? What do they call you?"

"When I was bangin' you I wasn't thinking about other women. I was only concerned with you, so other women shouldn't matter."

"Nigga fuck you!" she spat.

"Damn girl. All you doing is turning me on with this attitude of yours." Along with the smell of her hair, skin, and the warmth of her body. "A'ight look. I prefer that you call me Calvin. When I'm with you that's who I am. I didn't want Briggen to scare you away. You appear to be a good girl."

She laughed even though she was pissed. "That's a good one. You know what? Y'all niggas ain't shit! Now let me go!" She punched him in his chest. "Big liar! That's who you are to me."

"A'ight. I deserve that, but I'm not letting you go until we talk."

"Talk about what? What is there to talk about? You got what you wanted. Talk!" She was practically screaming. "You wasn't trying to talk when I was paging you. You never even answered your cell phone. Talk? You didn't even call to say that I was a good piece of ass, let's do that again! Nigga, please! We don't have shit to talk about! Now let me go!"

"Are you going to at least let me apologize?"

"Let me go liar." She tried to squirm away.

"I'm not letting you go until you at least hear me out. I had to go out of town for some important business. And then as soon as I got back, I had to turn right back around and head back out that same night. You were on my mind, but business comes first. And that's not a lie. You think I was wrong for not telling you about Briggen but on the real, I like to see how women will act with Calvin. Most bitches are just tryna get paid. I apologize. Can we move on and you give me another chance?"

"Another chance? Why do you want another chance with me? Don't you have about three or four steady bitches? You probably got a wife! Or are you ready to lie about that too? Liar!"

"Where are you getting all this misinformation from?"

"I see you didn't answer me liar! Just let me go."

"Not until you talk to me."

"We're done talking," she snapped.

"We haven't talked enough. I understand you're mad, but why don't you have a seat over there in the VIP section. Let me holla at my boy and I'll be there in ten minutes. A'ight? Can I at least get that? I like you Shan, and I wanna make it up to you."

"I'm ready to go *now*." She heard Brianna clear her throat and

34

then felt her tapping her shoulder. Brianna was ear hustling on their entire conversation and didn't miss a word.

"Hi, I'm here with my girl Shan. My name is Brianna. Can we get a bottle of Moet while she's sitting over there waiting on you? The night is still young and plus I'm waiting on someone." She flashed a seductive grin.

"Anything your girl here wants is on the house." He squeezed her ass while enjoying the feel of the soft butter leather. "Shan, you looking good baby. Can you please wait ten minutes for me? Plus, your girl is *thirsty*." He said thirsty meaning a greedy gold diggin' bitch.

"Let me go."

"Ten minutes. Ten minutes?" He pleaded. When he heard her suck her teeth he turned her loose but then grabbed her hand, pleased that he got his way. "Let me take y'all over there."

As they walked through the club, anybody who was somebody was checking out who was in Briggen's company. Shan felt like a fool for not knowing who he was and disliked the attention, but Brianna was loving every minute of it. Shan made a mental note of the pack of rats moving across the room. They were grillin' her and Brianna so hard, she was sure that if looks could kill, she and Brianna would be dead and stinking. Shan pouted as Briggen led them to a table in the VIP section. She was caught by surprise when her feet sunk into the thick red carpet. Mirrors and candles were everywhere.

He looked into Shan's eyes. "You gonna wait here for me, right?"

"Ten minutes."

Just as the rat pack reached their table, Sharia spoke up. "Who the fuck is that hoe?" she said to her crew.

"Who?" her sister Demetria asked.

"That bitch with Briggen over at the VIP section, that's who!" Sharia snapped. Sharia was one of Briggen's girls.

All four pairs of eyes turned towards the VIP table that was now getting served a bottle of Moet and a bottle of White Zinfandel because Briggen knew that was what Shan liked to drink. Both bottles were sitting on a bucket of ice. When they saw Shan cross her arms and roll her eyes at Briggen, it was on.

"Who is that hoe?" Vicki asked as she snapped her neck and rolled her eyes. Vicki was Sharia's overprotective best friend.

"The bitch obviously got an attitude with him about something," Sharia said.

"Better you than me," Demetria added, pouring salt on an open wound while hatin'.

"I've seen that other hoe somewhere, but I can't place her," Nay Nay added.

Mad as that hoe is they done fucked, Sharia told herself. But knew she better not even think about confronting Briggen's crazy ass in public. "I'm so tired of this shit," she said to Demetria.

"You obviously ain't too tired, you're still with him." Demetria rolled her eyes at her sister. "And you know not to get me started. And don't you start no shit, either! See, look. He's gone."

"Bitch, you know he's coming back. That's why her hoe ass is sitting with her arms crossed. And look at her gold diggin' friend, guzzlin' down the free drinks."

"Aww, hell naw! Stop the motherfuckin' presses! Look who just sat down next to her friend!" Vicki practically jumped off her stool. "Where them hoes from?" She was getting mad jealous as Skye moved in close to Brianna.

"I believe y'all bitches are gonna make tonight very interesting," Demetria said. "Now pass me the dro and gimme a light!"

"Were you anxiously waiting for me to come and find you?" Skye asked Brianna as he moved his chair closer to hers.

"Waiting? Yes. Anxious? No." Brianna coolly answered. "Let me introduce you to my girl Shan. Shan this is Skye. Skye this is my girl Shan."

"What's up Shan?" He stared at her for a minute. "You're Peanut's little sister aren't you? You look just like that nigga."

She nodded her head yes. "Nice to meet you Skye." She halfheartedly commented. He noticed that she was watching the time and that she had a major attitude.

He turned his attention back to Brianna. "Whose table you got me sitting at? Ain't nobody gonna run up on me are they?" He grabbed her chair, turning it around and placing it directly in front of his so that now they were facing each other. He ran his hand up the outside of her thigh.

"Looks to me like you're not worried about anybody running up on you."

"You never know. Y'all know how y'all do. But it's on you. What's up Brianna? We can kick it here or we can leave. It is Brianna isn't it?"

"That's who I am. I see you did a little research."

"Fo' sho. So what's up Brianna?"

"I'd rather leave but me and my girl came together."

"Can't we drop her off? Then you can tell me where we can go."

"Let me talk to her." He slid his chair back so that she could get up.

Seeing B get up Shan asked, "Are we leaving now? I'm ready to go."

"Girlfriend, come here." Brianna pulled Shan up and away from the table. She peeked at her two-way, smiled, then asked, "You mind driving my car home?"

Placing her hand on her hip Shan snapped, "You leaving with him?"

"Yeah. I thought you was gonna wait for Briggen."

"Girl please. His ten minutes has now turned into fifteen. If you wasn't so anxious to sit in the VIP section and suck up free drinks, I could have been gone."

"I'll make it worth your while." She handed Shan the keys to her Lex and the valet stub.

"How is this supposed to be worth my while, hoe?"

"I'm a paid hoe! Now drive my Lex and I'll give you all the details."

"Be careful." Shan rolled her eyes at her girl. Brianna turned away and grabbed onto Skye and didn't look back.

Once outside Brianna said, "Thanks for walking me outside. Something came up that I need to take care of. Can I get a rain check?" She seductively smiled at him.

"You owe me more than a rain check." His left eyebrow raised.

"A'ight then. Just let me know." Brianna was glad that Skye gave her the perfect alibi to leave the club and her car with Shan.

Just then a fully loaded burgundy Yukon pulled up and one of the lightly tinted windows came down. "Yo, B! C'mon." Peanut yelled, making eye contact with Skye.

"Oh, it's like that?" Skye asked her, not taking his eyes off of Peanut.

"Rain check," she mouthed at Skye as she got into the Yukon.

Skye stood watching as they pulled off. He pulled out his celly while going to his ride. "Ain't this a bitch!" he mumbled.

Shan grabbed her Coach bag and headed towards the bathroom. She spotted Briggen talking to two of Memphis' finest, Six-Nine and Tareek. They made eye contact and he waved her over. When he saw that she wasn't coming he excused himself and went to catch up with her. He was watching where Shan was going and Sharia was watching where he was going.

"I knew they were fucking." Sharia said to no one in particular. "Damn. I promised myself I wouldn't do this shit no more. If he don't give a fuck, then why should I?"

"That's what I've been tryna tell you for the longest. Don't say you've finally seen the light?" Demetria teased.

"Yeah, fuck it! The more I beat bitches' asses for messing with him, the more they come around. Then he looks at me like I'm in the wrong." Sharia said, not taking her eyes off of Briggen.

"I know you saw me wave you over," Briggen said as he grabbed Shan by the hand.

"I'm going to the ladies' room and then I'm going home. Your ten minutes was up ten minutes ago. However, I will allow you one phone call."

"Damn. When can I call?" He was trying to not get pissed knowing that he wanted to fuck her again. But at the same time, she just showed him that she still wanted to play.

"It doesn't matter."

"It doesn't matter? What kind of answer is that? Obviously I must be on your shit list." He leaned towards her to kiss her on the lips and she turned her head. "I'm reduced to a kiss on the cheek?"

"Call me."

"Let me walk you to your car."

"I'll be all right. Go finish doing what you was doing. Call me."

Sharia was sitting at the table watching as they parted ways. As soon as Shan came out of the bathroom Sharia jumped up and followed her to the front of the club. She couldn't help herself. Briggen was an addiction. The only thing she said to her crew was, "Let me go check on something. I'll be right back." They didn't even hear her because they were running to the dance floor to jam to Mr. Cheeks, Missy Elliott, and Petey Pablo.

When she caught up with Shan, she tapped her on the shoulder. "Excuse me. Excuse me." As soon as Shan turned around Sharia punched her in the face. "Bitch, Briggen is already taken!" Still catching Shan by surprise she punched her again. Shan slipped and fell backwards onto a table where Sharia was able to really whip her ass. Sharia blanked out as she threw continuous punches on every unprotected area of Shan's body. When they pulled Sharia off Shan, her nose was bleeding, her necklace was gone and the buttons on her leather jacket were dangling.

"Where's my fuckin' purse?" Shan screamed. "You skank bitch!" She lunged at Sharia. "I don't even know you!" she yelled as she tried to break away from Dino the bouncer.

"I'm Sharia, hoe! And Briggen is my man of three years. This is my club hoe! You will show me some fuckin' respect!" Sharia's size 38C's were heaving up and down. Her and Shan's eyes locked as their gazes were full of contempt and rage. Sharia's gaze wrestled with ego and humiliation.

Shan saw Briggen coming their way. "Briggen, tell this big nigga to get his hands off of me."

"Let 'em both go." He told Dino the bouncer. He looked from Sharia to Shan. They were now the center of attraction. Shan especially, since the black lace Victoria's Secret bra that he bought her was in full view.

"Calvin, find my fuckin' purse and my necklace," Shan ordered. Her chest heaving up and down.

"She called you Calvin?" Sharia was really hurt by that. "How can you disrespect me like this?"

"You need to train this ugly bitch!" Shan lashed out. Of course she didn't mean it because Sharia was downright beautiful. From the doe-shaped eyes, long eyelashes, and the radiant tan skin tone, she could easily give the actress Meagan Good a run for her money. Running up on Sharia and grabbing her by the hair, she said, "Bitch, I fucked your man; you need to show *me* some respect!" She got a punch in before Luke, the other bouncer, lifted her up into the air.

Briggen grabbed Sharia. "Go into the office and get yourself together." Shan was able to get in another punch as she grabbed Sharia's blouse, ripping it open. Then again, getting a fistful of Sharia's hair.

"Let her hair go Shan." Briggen was pulling on her fingers until Sharia's hair was freed.

Sharia burst out crying. "What is up with her Briggen? Who is she to you? I'm so tired of this shit!"

"Go into the office, now, Sharia!" Briggen ordered.

Dino the bouncer, put his arm around her and was guiding her towards the office. She tried to break away and get in her man's face. "What's up with her Briggen? How long have you been fuckin' her?" she screamed.

He gave Dino a look. When he did that, Dino picked her up and took her into the office. When he turned around Shan slapped him across his face. "Muthafucker, you got me twisted!" When she went to slap him again he grabbed her arm.

"Here's your bag. I'll replace the necklace. Come on; let me get you outta here. And slap me again, I'ma slap you back. You got *me* twisted."

"You can't replace the necklace! That was my mother's necklace. I want my necklace Briggen." Shan was so mad she didn't know what to do with herself. "You are bad news and a fuckin' trick and a liar!" she yelled at him as she scanned the floor for her necklace.

"I told you I'll replace the necklace. Now let me get you outta here."

"And I told you, you can't replace it. My mom gave that to me the night before they went on their trip. She told me to hold it until she got back. But she never came back. They died that next day. I gotta have that necklace."

"Bitch!" Sharia screamed as she was running towards Shan with a switchblade. Luke was able to stop her and take it from her.

"C'mon Shan. I need to get you outta here. I told you that I'll get your necklace."

"No, that crazy bitch didn't come after me with a blade!" Shan held her chest in disbelief as they walked out the club and headed around to the rear parking lot. She kept looking back, expecting to see Sharia.

"Where's your car?" He was pulling her.

"How could you do this to me? I thought you had your shit together nigga. I'ma get you back for this." She couldn't seem to calm herself down.

"Where's your car?" They were walking around the parking lot. Shan was so busy cussing she wasn't even looking for the car. He grabbed her by her shoulders, shaking her. "Where is your car?" he repeated.

An all-white Beamer pulled up next to them as they were walking around the parking lot. When the window rolled down Mia said, "Baby, what's going on? And who in the fuck is she?"

"Who are you?" Shan stopped in her tracks and went over to the Beamer; adrenaline still pumping, full blast, Shan was really confused now because this bitch looked just like Sharia. Briggen picked her up and she kicked the door, scraping it with her heel. "Who am I?" she screamed. "I'm the bitch he took to Las Vegas and fucked three weekends ago. Did you know that?"

Mia couldn't even get a sentence formed. Finally she said, "No, this crazy bitch didn't just scrape my door and tell me she spent a whole weekend fucking my man! Did you hear her Tanya?"

"Yeah, I heard her. Now watch where the fuck ya going! You almost hit that car!" Tanya yelled while reaching for the steering wheel.

Mia didn't even hear her. "Who is she Briggen?" She was driving slow and right up on them.

"I just told you who I am," Shan spat.

"Go home Mia. I'll be there in a few!" Briggen yelled.

"I'm not going no-fuckin'-where. Who is this bitch?" Mia was looking at Shan whose nose was bleeding, lip was busted and she was looking like a madwoman.

"Go home now, Mia! I'm not going to say it again."

"Yeah, go home now, Mia, because tonight it's my turn!" Shan screamed. "He's coming home with me."

"I know you're not going home with her!" Mia put the car in park and fast as lightning she was out.

What the fuck? Briggen said to himself. *It has to be a full moon. I'ma have to put my foot in this hoes ass.*

"Calvin, Brianna left. You're gonna have to take me home." She smirked at Mia and she crossed her arms across her chest, standing close to Briggen.

Mia ran over to Shan and swung on her. Her fist landed on her left jaw. "That's for scraping my door!" Before Briggen could stop her she sprayed Shan's face with mace. "That's for fucking my man!" She then went to beating Shan's ass. Dino the bouncer was now outside with them. Mia was small but quick. She was trying to stomp Shan into the ground. Shan was coughing and choking from the mace while trying to cover herself from Mia's feet. Briggen was too busy coughing and gagging. Dino finally grabbed up Mia while Briggen managed to pick up Shan, breaking the two females apart. He carried her to his clean, black, fully loaded Denali. He practically threw her inside, went over to Mia, grabbing her in a choke hold.

"Take your ass home Mia! Let me handle my business." He was still coughing.

"Who is she Briggen?" She tugged at his shirt. "Why the fuck are you taking her home?" He opened her car door and pushed her inside. She tried to get back out. He grabbed her by the neck and squeezed. "I'm not going to tell you again," he threatened and pushed her down into the car, then slammed the door. When she opened the door he punched her in the face.

"Come on. Get out," he dared her.

Dino handed him a wet towel and the necklace. "Dino man, make sure she leaves."

Dino nodded. "I got her."

"I hate you!" Mia was crying and screaming.

Briggen went and opened the door to his Denali, where Shan was gagging and crying. He gave Shan the cold wet towel for her face, then went around the driver's side, slid the necklace under the backseat, and jumped in.

6

FOREVER

It was 8:20 Saturday morning and Forever was finally dressed in his beige khaki visit uniform. He had spent all morning overseeing the perfect pressing of his uniform, the shining and polishing of his boots and the precise trimming of his goatee. The only thing he forgot was some picture tickets. He was impatiently walking back and forth in his cell waiting to be called to go to the visiting hall. He hadn't held his woman or daughter in over eight months.

Nyla, on the other hand, was waiting impatiently in the visitors' processing area with Tameerah who couldn't be still. "Mommee, is it our turn to go in yet?" she asked for the fifth time.

"Not yet, baby. In a minute."

Nyla thought to herself, *In a minute. In a minute. Everything for the last five years has been hoped to be over in a minute.* She would ask Forever, "Baby, when are you coming home?" His answer would be, "In a minute." "When will we be able to live like a family?" "In a minute." She was so sick of that phrase. "In a minute!" But being the strong, loyal, and dedicated black queen that she was, she had to show strength and stay positive. For the last five years every weekend she was in line by 7:45 A.M. to see Forever. So she told herself that she needed to go ahead and put on her game face. Not only for herself, but for Tameerah and Forever as well. But today, unfortunately, wearing that game face was kind of hard. She just wasn't feeling it. And it was most likely because she got her period in the middle of the night. She was pissed, especially since today she was planning on getting some dick. She was just telling her sister Lisha that eight months was a helluva long time to go without. Lisha's reply was, "Hell, yeah! Ain't no way I wouldn't be getting some dick on the side! You crazy, girl!"

Nyla was feeling crazy hot last night. After she put Tameerah to bed she ran herself a nice hot tub of water filled with oil and bubbles. She missed Forever so much and he sounded so good when she heard his voice earlier that she wished she could have jumped through the phone. Her pussy was on fire and her fingers were not getting the job done. This was one of those times that she wanted Forever so bad that it hurt. She used the back of her hand to wipe the tears away as she prayed for strength. But it seemed like the more she prayed the harder the throbbing got between her legs. Not being able to take it anymore she turned the water on, allowing it to flow at a nice warm temperature before scooting up, leaning back and placing her feet up on the walls. As the warm cascade of liquid ran over her pussy she imagined Forever's dick making long deep thrusts while constantly rubbing against her clit. "Sssssss," Nyla moaned out. "Forever, I love you." She groaned as the water beating against her clit and pussy opening brought her to orgasm. She scooted back, breathing hard as she began to cry. She couldn't even ask, "What part of the game is this?" Because she already knew. So she turned the water off, pulled out the stopper and got out.

"Thompson!" The processing officer yelled, interrupting her thoughts.

"It's about time," Nyla mumbled as she glanced at her watch. It was 8:50. She had been at the prison since 7:45. "Come on baby." She grabbed Tameerah's hand as they headed for the front desk.

In the visiting hall Forever was pacing back and forth, anxiously waiting for his family. Ten minutes later when the first group of visitors came through the doors he heard, "Daddee, Daddee!" Tameerah yelled happily as she jumped into Forever's arms.

"Tameerah, look how big you are. You're almost bigger than me!" he teased as he smothered her face with kisses.

"No I'm not!" She giggled as he tickled her. "Daddee, today are you coming home with us? Me and Mommee want you to come home."

"I know baby. I want to come too. In a few, I'll be there. We got to wait a few more minutes. We can do that, right?"

"I want you to come home today," Tameerah whined. "Why can't you come today? You want me to ask the man Daddee?"

Forever felt his chest heave and stomach knot up. Nyla had to use all the strength she had to hold back the tears as Forever explained to Tameerah why he couldn't go home with them today. It took Forever a good fifteen minutes of negotiating with his daughter and getting her into a positive mindset.

Finally, Tameerah nodded her head yes and hugged him around his neck. "Can I go play with the toys now?"

"Toys?" Forever teased. "I thought you came to see your daddy."

Tameerah giggled. "I did. But I'm ready to go play with the toys. I'll be right back to play with you. Okay?" She took off but ran back and said, "I gotta tell you about my rabbit too!"

Forever sighed, acting like he was disappointed. "I'll be waiting. Give Daddy a kiss." She kissed him on the cheek. "Give Daddy another kiss." He kissed her on the lips and then gave her another one on the nose.

"Daddee!" She laughed.

"Okay. I'ma let you go. You coming back, right?" She nodded her head yes. "You gotta tell me about school and Mr. Rabbit."

She laughed. "That's not his name. I'll be right back." She squirmed away and he breathed a sigh of relief as he watched her run over to the toys.

"Excuse me Miss, can I have a hug?" Forever had turned around and smiled at the woman who had been by his side for the last seven years. She was seated with her legs crossed and was looking up at him. She was fine just like Halle Berry. Petite, same complexion and even had a similar haircut. He walked over to her. "Come here girl." He pulled her up out of the chair. "I miss you so much." He gave her a big hug.

"How much you wanna bet I miss you more?" She ran her hands up and down his back as she eased her warm tongue between his lips and melted in his arms.

Forever came up for air. *"Mmmm,"* he moaned. "That kiss said you do miss me more." He guided her over to one of the big round poles and leaned her up against it. There were couples all around them trying to get a little something off before the visiting room officer told them to sit down. "Why do you have these pants on?" He pinched her butt cheek. "It's been eight months since you've been down here and you show up wearing pants? What's up baby?"

"What do you think is up? I got my period sometime during the night."

"Damn Ma."

She teasingly smacked the back of his head. "Nigga what? You ain't the only one who hasn't been fucked in eight months!"

"Watch your mouth girl," he told her as he put her hand on his dick, which was already hard. As he simultaneously watched out for the visiting officer and played with her nipple she stroked his dick. "Damn, that feels good."

"Does it," Nyla said, more as a sexy comment than a question. She felt him grow harder. "How good?"

Forever sucked her lips. "So good that if you don't stop we're gonna have an accident." He reached down and moved her hand. "Give me another kiss." She stood on her tiptoes and gave him a kiss. She gave a few subtle grinds on that hard dick. Forever said, "Ma, you're gonna have to slow it down. You're starting something that we can't finish."

"I can finish it. You want me to finish it for you?" She was kissing him all over his neck.

"You know I do. Tell Daddy how you're gonna finish it."

"You can't hit the walls but I can work the jaws."

Forever smiled. "That's why you're my baby. Now tell me how much you miss this big tasty dick."

"Let these guards blink their eyes and I'll show you how much I miss this big tasty dick." She went to unzip his zipper.

"Daddee, Daddee! I'm back!" Tameerah was yelling.

"Party's over for the time being." Forever kissed Nyla again as she zipped him up. Then he turned to Tameerah. "What took you so long? I've been waiting on you," Forever said as he went and picked Tameerah up.

After an hour of playing with her dad and half an hour of eating microwave fish, fries and candy, Tameerah crawled up into her dad's lap and went to sleep.

"Finally," Nyla mumbled.

"Where does she get all of this energy?" Forever asked as he leaned over and kissed Nyla on the cheek.

"Puhleeze. You haven't seen anything. Spend a day with her. Like all day Saturday or a Sunday!"

"I'm actually looking forward to doing that. So . . . What's up with you? You've been mighty quiet most of the day. You seemed to be a'ight over the phone. I thought you would be glad to see me. Come here." He leaned forward and playfully bit her lip. "What's up with you? What's on your mind?"

She played in Tameerah's hair, not saying a word. Forever waited a few more minutes before asking her again. "Baby you gonna talk to me or what?"

"I'm just tired, Forever. I'm PMSing so of course that's not helping none. I'm tired of you being in here. I'm tired of our daughter asking when are you coming home. I'm tired of you going to the hole. I'm tired of talking to you over the phone. I'm tired of sleeping in my bed every night all by myself. I'm tired of using my fingers. I'm just tired of being tired. Some days are much harder than others. And today is one of them *very* hard days. Shit Forever, I know you don't think this is easy for me?"

"What?" Forever asked incredulously and was shocked at the same time. "What the fuck you tryna say, Nyla?"

"Why are you raising your voice Forever?"

"Don't tell me how loud to fuckin' talk! What are you tryna say? Spit it out!"

Nyla sucked her teeth and rolled her eyes. "Forever today is not the day. I said what I had to say. I'm just tired, okay? I'm tired of our situation. I *know* that I can get tired sometimes. I'm human Forever."

"You're human." Forever's voice dripped with sarcasm. "So, what, you tryna move on to the next nigga? You gonna wait to the end of the bid to flip the script on me?" Forever threw his hands up in the air in exasperation. "Ain't this some shit!"

"You didn't hear me say shit about moving on to the next nigga. Why are you jumping to conclusions Forever? This ain't the first time I said I was tired of this shit and damn sure won't be my last!" Nyla snapped back. "I use to be able to share my feelings with you. But the way you trippin', trust and believe that won't happen again." She turned her back to him.

Forever fixed his gaze on her while at the same time attempting to digest what she'd said. Yeah, she'd said she was tired many times before but this time she seemed full of resolve. And fuck the macho shit! Nyla was his life. He damned sure wasn't gonna lose her to the next nigga.

"Nyla." He tugged at her elbow. She sucked her teeth and moved farther away from him. "Baby."

"What Forever?"

"I'm sorry."

"This shit *ain't* easy, Forever."

"I know it's not easy. Have you forgot that we're doing this time together? You think I like being separated from my family? You think I don't worry about you being out there all by yourself? You think I like being able to see y'all only on the weekends, and under these conditions? Can't get a decent hug, kiss, or feel without niggas being all in your face or telling you to back up! And the hole? I know you don't think I like going to the hole. You know that's not voluntary; I have to make money to take care of my family. I know I can get some credit for doing that. And I know you don't think I like the fact that you sleep alone at night. It fuckin' kills me that I can't be there with you and my baby. So baby, keep in mind, the three of us are going through this together. We all are tired but at least we are counting down. A year and a half left. If you did five I know you can do a year and a half more." He put his arm around her. "So what, you givin' up on us?" Nyla wiped the tears from her eyes and shook her head no. "We're counting down now, right?" She shook her head yes. "We can do these few more months can't we?" She shook her head yes.

7

SHADEE

When Shadee stepped inside his house it dawned on him that they might have left Hook's car parked on the street. "Born, call Teraney and tell him to make sure that nigga's car is gone."

"What was he driving?"

"I don't know man. Just make sure it ain't out there," Shadee snapped.

"Tell him to look for that gray Mustang or Rob's black Explorer. I'm sure Hook didn't drive that dark brown Navigator," Timmy said.

"A'ight," Born responded as he picked up his cell phone.

Shadee went in the back to shower and change clothes. When he came back into the living room Timmy was asleep in the chair. Born was smoking a blunt and Slim had just got there.

"How you feelin' nigga?" Slim asked as he stretched out his long narrow legs and popped the cap on a forty.

"Man, I'm a'ight, I'm livin'. But y'all niggas got me fucked up, smokin' and drinkin' all up on my Italian leather furniture. Boy, put that shit out!" He threw a towel at Born.

"So what's the plan?" Slim wanted to know.

Shadee sat down next to Born. "I need a breather. I'ma snatch up Janay and chill out for a few."

"How long you plan on being gone?" Slim was countin' them dollars in his head. "We need to re-up. You said you was gonna have that cat from Dyersburg serve you up this time. He got dat shit."

"On my way back I'll stop and do that."

"On your way back?"

"Hell, yeah. On my way back," Shadee emphasized. "Y'all work with what y'all got. Then get served by your connect. It's your call. I'm giving you a chance to make some money."

"A'ight then. But if you need me to meet up with you, just page me."

Shadee nodded his head. "Wake that nigga up! This ain't no hotel."

Born kicked Timmy on his knee. "Wake up man! It's time to bounce!" Born kicked him again. Timmy woke up grabbing his piece.

"Nigga what you think you gonna do with that?" Born laughed.

"Stop playin' boy!" Timmy put his piece away, stood up and stretched.

"Boy? I get more pussy than you, punk! Now who the boy?" Born pounded his chest emphasizing that he was indeed the man.

"You better get this stank ass kid before I hurt him," Timmy told Shadee.

"I don't have time for y'all's shit." Shadee had his ear glued to the phone. He threw the phone down and mumbled, "Where this hoe at?"

"Man, that hoe Bri got you sprung," Born teased.

"Fuck you punk. Who said I'm calling her? As a matter of fact, all y'all get the fuck out. And while y'all at it, call Doc and tell him I'm waitin' on him."

"You got that Unc," Born said as he grabbed his phone. "But yo, I know you gonna handle her, right?"

"Oh yeah. I got something real nice planned for that bitch." She gonna wish that they killed my black ass when it's all said and done." Everyone nodded their heads in approval. Shadee stood up and opened the front door. "A'ight niggas. I'll holla at y'all." Everybody stood up except for Born. "You too nigga!" He pointed at Born.

"Come on Unc. Let me spend the night. Look at your head. You might faint or something."

"Lil' Nigga, get the fuck out. I ain't babysittin' tonight." Everybody started laughing.

Born reluctantly stood up. "A'ight Unc. I'ma remember this."

"Remember this and get the fuck out!" Everybody walked out except for Born, who stood in the doorway.

"Seriously. You gonna be a'ight?"

"I'm straight Lil' Nigga. I'll holla at ya!" He gave Born dap and closed the door.

Two hours later Doc was at the door. His arm was bandaged up and in a sling. Jo Jo was behind him carrying the dope and the money. Shadee took the money and put it up. He checked his dope and then told Jo Jo to handle it. He then told them that he was going away for a few and that he would be in touch.

The three of them headed out the house together. Jo Jo and Doc on their way to sell some dope and Shadee on his way to Janay's. The sun was just peeking above the horizon.

Janay was Shadee's wifey and his baby's mother. Janay's father, Big Choppa, used to be the man—that was until all the New Jacks began to spring up, including Shadee. So a stranger to the hustling game Janay was not. When Big Choppa was diagnosed with liver cancer, it was Janay who held his business down. But Shadee and Big Choppa never could get along. Janay had been hustling before she met Shadee. And of course he convinced her to stop, and Big Choppa didn't like that one bit. Big Choppa was always in and out of the hospital and Janay was always back and forth in the game. Even after she gave birth to Shadee's son Marquis, she kept on hustling. Finally Shadee said, "Enough is enough!" He was hustling enough for the both of them so he made her stop. When

Marquis was coming up on his second birthday, Janay was at it again. When Shadee found out he gave her an ass whipping that earned her a two-day stay in the hospital. But not before she shot Shadee in the arm.

Now three years later and still together Janay feels as if there is no other man for her and that she will forever be wifey and his number one ride-or-die chick. She has been by his side through the ups and downs, the highs and lows. She withstood all of the bitches trying to get with him. She stabbed one and shot another.

Janay and Shadee at one time was thick as thieves. But during the past six months he barely slowed down to spend time with her or their son. They both had to admit that their bond wasn't as tight anymore. But now, if Shadee had a clue what Janay had been up to for the last couple of months he probably would put a bullet through her skull. Every time he needed to get away he would take her with him except for the one time he took Brianna. When he pulled up in front of her house he started cursing because her car was parked in the driveway; he had been calling her but she wasn't answering the phone. He parked his car behind hers, got out and rang the doorbell.

After about two and a half minutes Janay was standing in front of him giving off much attitude. "Why do you think you have a key Shadee?" She rolled her eyes at him and left him standing in the doorway. "And what happened to your head?"

"I wasn't sure if I should use it. You wasn't answering the phone and I wasn't sure if you had company," he replied, ignoring the question about his head.

Janay stopped dead in her tracks and did what the sisters do when they put that hand on a hip and snap that neck back. "Nigga, don't even try it. That's something that you would do, not me. If I was to do something like that, trust and believe the locks would be changed and I would have the decency to tell you it's over. So just because you're guilty as fuck don't try to flip the script."

"I'm not flippin' the script. I just wanted to know why you wasn't answering the phone. I don't feel like fighting with you right now."

Pissed because he was remaining so calm, Janay walked away. She wanted to start an argument. Figuring she would give it one more try she stopped and turned around and asked, "If that's all you wanted to know, Shadee, then why didn't you just ask?" She went into the bathroom and started her bath water. When she came back into the living room she said, "Did it even occur to you that I was asleep? Just because you're out there fuckin' around doesn't mean that you have to be so suspicious of me."

Shadee seeing that she was in an arguing mood said, "I don't know what the fuck is wrong with you but you need to chill the fuck out. I'm going away for a couple of weeks and I want you and Marquis to come with me." He peeked in Marquis's room and saw that it was empty.

She sucked her teeth. "I gotta go to work Shadee. I just can't jump up and leave for weeks at a time. I do have a job."

"A job? What the fuck you got a job for? You on some bullshit now. I'm not making you work and you know that you don't have to work. So go 'head with that. As a matter of fact, quit that fuckin' job! You ain't doin' shit but wasting time. Time that you could be spending with our son. He still at your mom's?"

Janay snapped her neck back so hard it could have popped out its socket. "Our son? I can't tell it's our son! And where the fuck have you been? How do you think I feel when our son asks where is his father? Or, when will my daddy come home?"

"I got Marquis. Don't worry about our relationship."

"What the fuck is that supposed to mean?" Janay's mouth hung open in disbelief. "You know what? No. Forget it. I don't have the energy." She waved him off.

He watched her long slender frame and flawless dark complexion walk away. Shadee loved tall women. She resembled supermodel Naomi Campbell. "And make sure you're ready tomorrow," he snapped.

She came out the bathroom wrapping a towel around her head. "And you can forget about me quitting this job. I want my own money."

"Girl, you are not pressed for money. What do you need?" He sat there staring at her. "Know what? I agree. We'll talk later. My head hurts and I need some sleep. Just make sure you and Marquis are packed and ready tomorrow night. And quit that fuckin' bullshit job!" He got up and left her standing there but wondered what was up with this new attitude.

When the phone rang, she didn't answer. Shadee turned around. "Who the fuck calling you this early? And why you ain't picking it up?" Her heart fell to the floor when he started for the phone.

"Hello."

The room was so silent that she heard the dial tone when the caller hung up. "Janay let me find out you creepin' with some nigga." He was eyeballin' her. "Who was that?"

"Shadee please. I've been getting that a lot lately," she said, turning to go to the kitchen where her cell phone was, while praying it didn't ring. "Of course you wouldn't know, you're never here, right?" She heard the bedroom door slam as she put her cell on vibrate. "What have I gotten myself into?" she mumbled.

8

SHAN

Briggen was silent as he drove. Shan was still recovering from her two beatdowns and the mace. When she got herself together she said, "I don't believe this shit." She grabbed her cell phone and called Brianna. When she didn't get an answer Shan dialed her house phone. The voice mail picked up. "Hey, it's me. Your car is still parked at the club. You need to go pick it up as soon as possible. If you would have stayed ten minutes longer your girl here wouldn't have gotten her ass beat. I knew I should have left when I started to." She put the cell phone away and looked into the mirror. "Look at my damn face! I have to go to work Monday. I can't go to work like this. I can't call out the first damn day!" She was practically screaming. Briggen pulled up in front of her house and before he could park Shan was outta the car and practically running towards her building.

Briggen jumped outta his truck, caught up to her and grabbed her arm. "Shan, hold up."

She snatched her arm away and headed for her building with Briggen on her heels. "Why are you following me? Go home to all of them crazy ass hoes who *need* you and obviously put up with your bullshit and leave me the fuck alone! I ain't the one Briggen." She was struggling to get the key in the lock but it wouldn't go in.

She could barely see because now she was crying again and mad as hell.

Briggen took the keys from her. "Let me do it."

"I don't think so," she snapped as she went to snatch them back. He held them up in the air so she couldn't reach them. "Give me my keys. Don't you think you've done enough for one night?" She tried to snatch them again. "Your motherfuckin' bitches are lucky I didn't have my gun on me."

Briggen stuck her key in the lock and stepped inside.

"Are you coming in?" He smirked as he went over to the couch and sat down.

She slammed the door shut, went into the bathroom and started some bath water. She went into the kitchen, grabbed a wineglass and a bottle of White Zinfandel, and took that into the bathroom. She then stripped, filled her glass up and immersed her sore body into the hot steaming water.

Briggen went out to his truck, got her necklace and his little travel bag and came back inside. He got comfortable as he took his time and rolled a blunt. *What a night,* he thought to himself, placing the philly blunt box back into the travel bag.

An hour later Shan was chillin' in the tub and feeling a little better. She allowed the steaming hot bath to soothe her aching bones and had downed two glasses of Zinfandel. She was drying off when the phone rang. She ran to it, hoping it was Brianna. "What's up hoe?"

Whoever it was hung up. Remembering that she had left Briggen in her living room she peeked her head around the corner. "Tell your bitches to stop calling my house and hanging up."

"I got your necklace." He ignored her sarcasm.

"Congratu-fuckin'-lations! I believe that's the least you can do, other than paying me for getting violated on your property. And what about my girl's car? Is it gonna be all right?"

"What was she driving? I'll have to call and tell them to keep an eye on it."

"It's a champagne colored Lexus. She watched him as he dialed his celly. As soon as he began to talk she got close enough to ear hustle. She heard him give instructions on keeping an eye on Brianna's Lex, asked what was up with Sharia and Mia—even though he didn't say their names, she knew what was up. And the last thing she heard was him inquiring about the total of all receipts for the night.

"You can set my necklace on the table and leave."

"Let me holla at you."

"Tomorrow."

"I gotta go out of town tomorrow."

Shan sucked her teeth and threw on her robe. The wine had her feeling real nice. Walking into the living room, Briggen was just sitting in the dark chillin'. She turned on the lamp. "Did you call them and tell them to keep an eye on her car? That quick?"

"Yes ma'am, I did."

She held her hand out for her necklace.

"You gonna let me apologize for tonight?"

"You can apologize; I'm listening."

He looked up at her. "Can you at least sit down for a minute? I'm not going to bite you. Please, sit down." Shan remained standing, crossed her arms and fixed her gaze onto Briggen.

"I'm sorry that everything went down the way it did. If you'll give me a chance I'll make it up to you. Are you all right? I am sorry, for real."

"You call that an apology? That's not good enough. But I'm not in the mood right now. I want you to leave."

"I thought you said you wanted me to apologize? What is your definition of an apology? What is it that you want?"

"Why did you fake like you was this serious businessman? You could have been straight with me and told me that you got your hustle on."

Briggen wiped his face with his hands before looking at Shan. "I am a businessman. All that other shit you accusing me of, that ain't me. I'm just a businessman trying to stay afloat. I like you

Shan. I don't have to lie to you. All my cards is always on the table."

"Bullshit Briggen! You said you was Calvin the businessman. A month later I find out you are Briggen the dope dealer. You call that laying everything on the table?"

"Shan, why—"

She cut him off. "As far as laying everything on the table—I saw you practice that when it comes to them hoes. They both seem to be very accepting of the fact that they are not the only one. At least the two I ran into tonight. How many more do you have?"

"It ain't what you're thinking Shan. They run my businesses."

"But you fuckin' them Briggen, and they are calling you their man. So, what? How many more are there?"

"I can't stop them from calling me what they want to call me."

Shan gave him the hand. "Cut the bullshit Calvin. Just leave. I'm too tired for this shit." Plus he was blowing her mind with them hoes being so accepting of the fact that they're sharing. She had to admit that the dick was good, but damn.

"You said I owe you for getting violated. Let's negotiate. You want this, don't you?" He held up her necklace, dangling it back and forth. When she saw her mother's necklace she let out a sigh of relief.

"A'ight. We can do this." Briggen pulled out his wallet. "How much we talking?" he wanted to know.

"First, I want a better apology." She sat down across from him.

"A'ight. I'm sorry for the way things went down tonight. I had no idea shit would happen the way it did. I was glad to see you, that's why I asked—or rather begged—you to stick around. I just wanted to kick it with you. I—"

Shan cut him off. "Why in the fuck do you want to kick it with me and you got all them other bitches!" She just couldn't get over that. "No! No!" She put her hand up. "Fuck it! Don't even answer that. Just give me my damn necklace and all the money you got on you. That'll make up for all the shit I went through tonight. And you better hope that I don't sue your ass! And you still didn't tell me how many hoes you got!"

"I thought you wanted me to apologize? How you gonna cut me off in the middle of the apology?"

"Nigga, cut the bullshit all right?" He could tell that she was really pissed off.

"A'ight. You got that." Briggen opened his wallet and pulled out all the bills. "I already told you those bitches run my businesses. One runs the club and the other one runs my day care center."

"Whatever nigga. I know it's another one running your car shop. Just toss the dough onto the coffee table," she ordered. "And I know you got a money clip. Pull that out! And you got another hoe trafficking your dope."

"Anything else, Your Highness?" Briggen asked as he did what he was told, not wanting to touch the fact that she was calling out all of his business. *Hoes talk too damn much*.

"Now give me my necklace." When he placed it in her hand, he tried to pull her up. "Don't even try it nigga. You are now dismissed."

"What if I told you I didn't want to go."

"That's your problem. Not mines." She stood up and he put his arms around her waist. "It's time for you to go. You know all your hoes are waiting on you."

"I'm here with you. You got me now." He was easing her back towards the couch.

"Briggen—or Calvin—don't even try it," her voice squeaked.

"Remember you told me, 'Briggen, I had been trying to reach you for days.' Well, here I am. What did you want? You got me."

"I was trying to reach Calvin not Briggen. I don't know who Briggen is."

"I'll tell you all about Briggen. Briggen has been feenin' for some of this pussy." he whispered as he bent down and kissed her lips. "What else do you want to know about him?" He kissed her again.

"Nothing . . . right now," she barely got out.

He sat down on the couch and pulled her between his legs. "You don't deserve me," she mumbled.

"I know baby." He raised one of her legs up and placed it on the couch. She grabbed onto his shoulders and was anticipating what was coming next. She held on tight as Briggen spread those pussy lips, pulled the hood up over that clit and went to sucking.

"You don't deserve me, nigga." She moaned as her clit grew harder and bigger. "Nigga, shit!" she yelled as she went to grinding against his tongue. "Brig, Cal, whoever the fuck you are, oh, nooooo, don't stop!" She screamed as she started to cum, digging her nails into his shoulders. Her juices were squirting out and Briggen was sucking it all up. "Oh, shit! Oh, shit!" She kept screaming as he brought on her second orgasm. She was enjoying his lips and tongue as they tickled her tingling body. He finally came up to her nipples where he sucked and teased them to the point where she was ready for round three. "Nigga go back to where you just came from," she ordered as she spread her sweaty, sticky thighs.

"Damn your pussy taste good." Briggen smirked as he slid two fingers inside of her and watched as she began to grind nice and slow. She gently placed both hands on his head, guiding him to where she needed him to be. Briggen, wasting no time, continued to finger fuck her as he began licking her clit.

"Babeeeeee. Oh, my God!" Shan cried out in ecstasy as she was trying to mash her pussy in his face. Oh, this feels sooo good. Right there, baby. Right there. Oh, my!" She tried to stop that tongue action but Briggen wasn't having it. "Oh, please!" she screamed out as her juices squirted every which way.

"See what you've been missing out on," Briggen sarcastically said as he stood up. When the flow stopped Briggen picked her up. She was limp as a rag doll. She hadn't cum since the last time they were together.

"Oh, shit!" she kept repeating as she caught her breath. He was moving towards her bedroom. "Hold up. Put me down." As soon as her feet hit the floor she closed her robe and tied it.

"Why are you tying it? Let's take it to the bedroom."

"Bedroom? I know you heard me. I said you didn't deserve me. Now get the fuck out!" She switched her ass to the door and swung it open. Briggen looked at her as if she was crazy. "That's right nigga! I said get the fuck out!"

Briggen just shook his head. "So it's like that?"

"Out, hoe! Nigga get the fuck out!"

When he reached the door he moved her hand off the knob and slammed it shut. "You got me fucked up. I'm not going anywhere. We gonna finish this."

She ran for her cell phone and dialed 911. "Now nigga, how do you want this to really end? With me or the police? Hello!" She said into the phone while staring at Briggen. "What's up?"

He smirked at her as he opened the door. "A'ight, you got that off."

"I did, didn't I? Bye."

Briggen shut the door behind him and stood there. When he heard her lock it he smiled at the thought of how he just got played big time. *That pussy was worth it.* He said to himself as he headed for his Denali, jumped in, and pulled off.

9

BRIANNA

Peanut looked over at Brianna and asked himself when was he going to stop fucking with her. He knew that the only reason he was asking himself that was because of the guilt he was temporarily feeling. Less than an hour ago he was at home chilling with wifey when Brianna two-wayed saying, "Let's finish what we started earlier. At Club Premiere. Come and get it, Daddy!" He told Keke he had to make a run and would be right back.

"What's up with the trucks?" Brianna teased, breaking his train of thought. "Everybody wants to drive a truck."

"For me, it's comfort. I'ma tall nigga. I'm hungry. Where do you wanna go?"

Brianna looked at her watch. "Not too many choices this time of morning. IHOP, CK's, Kettles."

"Well, you wanna go cook?"

"Cook? I didn't page you to cook. I wanna fuck!" she seductively answered.

"A'ight then." Peanut laughed. "I guess I'll pick the spot. 'Cause a nigga gots to eat first, then we can fuck." He headed for IHOP, cruising down American Way.

After Brianna ate blueberry pancakes and watched Peanut kill a sirloin steak, cheese omelet, potatoes and two glasses of Welch's grape juice, she was full. It was almost 3:00 A.M. when they headed for Bri's house.

"So what is your girl gonna say about you being out all night?"

Peanut grinned. "Since when have you gave a fuck?"

"All right smart ass. If you got it like that, then you can do it more often."

"Don't be greedy Ma. Plus, you start being greedy your girl Shan gonna peep game. Even though I still don't understand why you tryna hide the shit."

Brianna sucked her teeth. "Shan is my sister. I know her. And trust me when I say it, if she finds out that her best friend is fucking her brother neither one of us will ever hear the last of it."

"So what?" Peanut looked at her incredulously.

"Forget it. You don't understand."

"It ain't nothing to understand."

"Whatever. I don't want to argue with you about it."

"Well, let's argue about that nigga Skye you was with at the club. You fuckin' him?"

Brianna looked at him as if to say *Nigga, why you all up in mines?* She smirked before saying, "What if I was?"

"What the fuck you mean, 'what if I was?'" He smashed the side of her face up against the door window.

"Peanut, what the fuck is the matter with you?" she screamed in shock as she rubbed the side of her face. "No, I'm not fuckin' him! What is the matter with you? You questioning me? I don't bother you about wifey and whoever the fuck else you seein'!"

"That nigga is the enemy. Stay the fuck away from him. You feel me?"

This nigga got a lot of nerve. I don't believe this shit. He got a bitch at home and got the audacity to be checkin' me.

"Brianna?"

"I heard you Peanut." She was rubbing her face.

"I know you heard me but do you feel me?"

"I feel you, damn." She rolled her eyes at him. *This nigga done got me outta the mood. If the dick wasn't so good, I swear I'd pull out my switchblade. I can't believe he just did that.*

When they pulled in front of Brianna's, Peanut asked before he cut the engine off, "You want me to come up?"

She gave him that, *yeah, I wanna get fucked look* and said, "Oh, so now since you hit me you trippin'? Whatever." And she got outta the car.

"Oh, so now you mad?" Peanut answered as he shut off the engine. She ignored him and kept on going.

Once inside Brianna's apartment Peanut lit up a blunt and got comfortable listening to Brianna turn the shower on. He flipped through her CD collection and stopped at *Floetic* by Floetry. He was totally relaxed, had stripped down to his boxers and T-shirt and was damn near asleep by the time she came out the bathroom and straddled his lap.

"I know you didn't fall asleep on me," she whispered as she pulled his shirt over his head.

"Damn, you smell good. Like pears and peaches. Some shit like that. Stand up. Let me look at what you got on," he said, forgetting about the fallout they had earlier.

Brianna blushed as she stood up, knowing that she was the shit. She had on a see-through tan teddy with matching panties, garter belt, stockings, and mules to match. She played in her hair as she slowly twirled around for him.

"Bend over." He slid her panties down, spread her ass cheeks and went to licking her ass crack.

"Ooooh." Brianna shuddered as chill bumps popped up all over her body. At first it was tickling but then it began to feel good as her pussy began to juice up. "No . . . one . . . has ever . . . oh, my God . . . done . . . this . . . before . . . oooohsh . . ."

"Stay right there," Peanut mumbled as he pulled out a condom and put it on.

Brianna peeked behind her and her pussy got that much wetter as she looked at her favorite big dick. His dick so far was the biggest she'd come across. She tried to stand up. "Where do you think you're putting that?" she teased.

He gently pushed her back over. She grabbed onto the coffee table as he spread her legs. "You want Big Daddy, or what?" He put the head in her pussy and stopped.

"Oooh, yeah, give it to me Daddy," she moaned.

"I'll be gentle." He grabbed her hair, snapped her neck back and rammed all of his ten-and-a-half-inch dick inside her.

"P-P-P-Peanut . . . damn you . . ." Brianna moaned as he began to get his grind on. She liked for him to take that first entry slow. "Oh, shit! Slow down!" Peanut didn't want to but he did slow it down. He began making long in and out strokes. As Brianna was getting adjusted and was beginning to enjoy the feel of him inside her she could tell, as he was speeding up, that he was getting ready to cum. "Don't cum yet. Slow down baby," she pleaded.

"Slow down?" Baby I'm tryna stretch you out so we'll be straight for later on," he said as he began pumping harder, deeper, and faster.

Brianna tightened her grip on the coffee table. She felt like his dick was going to come up through her throat. "Nigga, shit!" She groaned as he started to cum.

He pulled her up by her hair and began sloppily kissing her on the neck. After he caught his breath he asked, "You a'ight?"

"Do not put one hickey on my neck," she said with much attitude.

"Don't be mad. I got you."

"When nigga? You got me all open and you done got yours."

Peanut laughed as he turned her around, kissed her on the lips and pulled her teddy up over her head.

"If only you fucked as good as you kissed I'd be a'ight," she snapped.

"Oh, really?" He picked her up and laid her on the coffee table.

"Peanuttt!" she shrieked. "This table is cold!" She tried to get up but he told her to lie back down as he pushed her legs up. "You better hope this table doesn't break." She giggled.

"It's not gonna break," he told her as he got on his knees and began fingering her and playing with her clit. She was no longer laughing as she widened her legs and put her legs across his shoulders. "Oh, you like this don't you?" He leaned over and began running his tongue all over her pussy.

"That's right nigga, show me what you got and return the favor from earlier." She moaned.

Peanut ate her pussy until she came and came again. Afterwards they took a shower together and ended up in the bed. With her on top and in control she was able to ride that dick in comfort until she came and his dick went limp.

"You straight now?"

"Mmmm-hmmm," she moaned as he sat up and began sucking on her nipples.

"I'm not straight. You gonna hook a nigga up again or what?" He planted soft kisses on her lips then got in position so that he could get some head.

"This is gonna cost you," she said, considering how big his dick was.

"You know you love this big dick."

He grabbed her by her hair and pushed her head down. "I want you to suck the head real nice for me," he ordered as he closed his eyes and laid back. Brianna was just getting into the groove when his cell phone rang. He motioned for her to keep going. He looked at the Caller ID and saw that it was wifey, Keke.

"Yo Brianna, if you can do this quietly keep going, if not, you're gonna have to excuse me while I take this call."

She stopped, looked at him and sucked her teeth. "Don't answer it. She'll call back."

"Keep it down, a'ight?" he warned as he answered the phone. "What up babee? How you doin'?"

Brianna took this opportunity to climb back on that long, hard dick and at the same time she was trying not to moan too loud.

"Hold up baby, let me turn this down." He pressed the mute

button on the phone. "Yo, get up! You too loud. Give me a few minutes, a'ight."

Brianna rolled her eyes. "You in my bed nigga!"

"But you ain't wifey! This here is my bitch on this phone yo." Brianna climbed off him, grabbed her robe and stormed out the room.

She walked to the living room, picked up her phone and dialed Shan's number. Her sleepy voice finally answered. "Hello."

"Hey girl, what's up?" Brianna said dryly.

"You don't sound like the hoe that snagged a baller last night. What happened? Things didn't go as planned? Where is he?" She yawned.

"Girl, please. Skye is here," she lied. "You know I never fail."

"What? He's asleep?" Shan was now sitting up in her bed, looking at the clock. It was six A.M.

"No. He's in there on the phone talking to his girl."

"His girl? Tell that nigga he can talk to her when he goes home!" Shan was practically yelling. "What's the matter with you B?"

"He let me know up front he had the hoe." She heard Shan suck her teeth. "Enough about me. What's up with you? What did you end up getting into last night?"

"Obviously you didn't check your machine B."

Shan now had Brianna's undivided attention. "Was I supposed to?"

"If you would've you would be aware of what all happened to me. Shit! I don't know where to start!"

"Start somewhere." Brianna was now staring at Peanut's hard, beautifully sculpted naked body and that long big dick was dangling. He was off the phone and leaned over and kissed her on the cheek.

"Come on back to bed Shorty." He kissed her on the lips. She rolled her eyes at him.

"Shan give me a minute." Before she could say anything he was sucking on her lips and her tongue.

"Let me finish this call okay?" She smiled at him.

"Hurry up." He kissed her again. "A'ight?"

"Okay." She was looking at his dick, which was now sticking straight out. After he turned and walked away she said, "Shan, girl, you just don't understand what some good dick will make a bitch do."

"No. I don't. And I really don't want to hear what you will do for some. Are you gonna listen to me or what?"

Shan ran down all of the events of the evening. From the two ass whippings to her leaving her Lexus at the club, to Briggen coming home with her, him giving her some head and her putting him out.

"Girl you are lucky Briggen didn't beat your ass for pullin' a pimp move like that! But back to my car, Shan. Go get my car please. You better hope my car is right where I left it. I can't believe you left my ride!"

"He has somebody watching it."

"Brianna!" Peanut was ready to get sucked.

She covered up the mouthpiece. "I'm coming." Getting back to Shan she warned her, "You better hope he do. Go get my car hoe. I need to get my hair done. I'll talk to you later." Brianna heard the shower start and got up and headed towards the bathroom. "How you gonna rush me off the phone then jump in the shower?"

"You took too long," he said, stepping into the shower.

"Don't make me hurt you nigga. Now *you* hurry up." She stormed out the bathroom. When she went into her bedroom she heard a cell ringing, and it wasn't hers. She felt around in his jean pockets and grabbed his phone.

"Hello."

"Who dis?"

"Who you lookin' for?"

"Put Nut on the phone."

Brianna sucked her teeth on her way to the bathroom. "You got a call."

"What?" he yelled over the water.

"You got a call."

He snatched the curtain back. "What the fuck you doing answering my phone?"

"You want me to have him call back?"

He cut the water off and stepped out, grabbing the phone from Brianna.

"What's up?"

Brianna began drying him off while trying her best to hear both sides of the conversation. Whoever Peanut was talking to was loud as shit, and even though they were talking in code she knew the lingo. Her pussy was getting wet at the thought of all that dope and money Peanut was getting ready to come up on. The next thing you know she was on her knees swallowing his cum.

"Aaah, shit," he groaned as Brianna was now sucking on his nuts. "You know what to do to keep from getting an ass whipping don't you. Get up."

She had a devilish grin on her face as she planted kisses on his chest and neck.

By nine that morning Brianna had been joyriding that dick and had cum about three more times before getting all the pieces of info to this big drop that he was getting ready to do. And as an extra bonus on his way out the door he dropped a grand on her coffee table.

Hours later when Brianna finally woke up she had Shadee on her mind and was wondering why he hadn't called her. This triggered instant paranoia. "Fuck! I know Hook didn't tell him I set him up." She sat up and debated on whether she should call him or not. "Shit!" Her heart was pounding as she grabbed her phone and dialed. "Hey, you!" She was trying hard to conceal her nervousness. "I started to hang up."

"What's up, B?" He yawned. "What did I do to deserve this call?" he teased. There was no doubt in anybody's mind that he had feelings for Brianna. Even Janay knew that.

"Don't even try it, nigga!" She relaxed a little. "You said you was coming over last night."

"What time is it?"

"It's almost 11:00. You comin' over?"

I can't believe this bitch is acting like she ain't did shit! "I doubt it. I gotta go out of town."

She got quiet. She knew that his out of town was to re-up. "When are you heading back?"

"In a couple of weeks."

All of her paranoia was gone now. "You said the next time you go away you was taking me," she pouted.

"You can't go this time B." *This hoe is really playing the role.* "I'll holla at you when I get back."

"When you get back? Can't you send for me?" she whined.

"I'll see." He heard her suck her teeth. "A'ight?"

"Okay. Bye." She had to hurry and get ready for her hair and nail appointment.

Shadee got up, showered and dressed. He had not forgotten how Janay had been acting. She was totally out of character but at the time he was in pain and too tired to find out what the fuck was her problem. So he figured he would ease up to this job, that all of a sudden she acted like she just had to have, take her to lunch and see what was up. He had a slight headache but told himself it was nothing that a hit of dro couldn't cure.

At 12:45 he was pulling up to her workplace. As he found a space to park he saw her come out of the building and look around. He paused when he saw a high yellow brotha step out of a black 745 BMW and wave her over. "What the fuck?" He cursed as he started the car. *Honk! Honk! Screeech!* The truck next to him cut him off before he pulled out of his parking space. "Damn!" When he looked up Janay was looking at him. He saw her lean into the Beamer and shortly after it pulled off. Shadee jumped out of his car so fast he damn near got hit by a bus. Janay was calmly walking to meet him.

Before he could get up on her he yelled, "You didn't have to tell your little nigga to pull off and cancel your date just because I pulled up. You should have fuckin' introduced us!"

"That wasn't a date."

"Then why in the fuck did you get scared and tell him to leave? Who in the fuck was he? That's the nigga that called this morning, wasn't it?"

"Why are you yelling?" Janay was getting embarrassed because people were beginning to stare.

"Bitch. Who in the fuck do you think I am?" He smacked her. Then he snatched her up by her throat. Noticing how everybody was all up in their mix, he turned her throat loose but held onto her collar. "Who do you think you fuckin' with? Who the fuck am I to you!"

Janay shook her head in disbelief. "I don't believe you! You sure are mighty possessive for a nigga who is creepin' nonstop." She tried to snatch away but he took one hand and began squeezing her neck.

"Who the fuck is he?"

"Turn me loose, Shadee. You're making a scene and here comes the police." Shadee still held on tight. "Babee, turn me loose."

"Is everything all right ma'am?" the short officer with the mustache asked.

Janay had grabbed Shadee by the waist and pulled him close.

"Everything's okay, officer. Thank you," she said sternly to the officers.

"Y'all have a nice day." He stood watching them as they walked away.

After they got out of earshot, she grabbed Shadee's face. "Listen to me. You my nigga. I know that, so does everyone else. I'm not fuckin' nobody else. I need you to trust me. Just because you got other bitches don't mean I have other niggas. Now look at you. You having a fit because you think I'm fuckin' somebody else. It don't feel good do it? But you know what? You a dog

Shadee and a dog always finds his way home. But right now, I'm handling something. So you are going to have to let me handle mines. You keep doing you and let me do me. A'ight?"

"Girl, you got one second to tell me what the fuck is going on!"

The Beamer pulled up beside them. Before Shadee could say a word she slipped her tongue inside his mouth. She pulled back and said, "I told him to circle around the block because I had to holla at my man. I'll meet you at the house around six. I'm already packed." She kissed him again. "I gotta run." She hurried and jumped into the Beamer. Shadee stood there speechless.

"Sha, I'm so glad you sent for me," an excited Brianna cooed as she jumped into the rented Suburban that Shadee was driving. The Atlanta sun was bouncing off the hood. Brianna smiled as she slid her Gucci shades on the top of her head and kissed Shadee on the cheek. "I'm down in the dirty dirty South! Can we go to Club One Tweezy tonight?" Brianna was practically bouncing up and down.

"I don't know, depends on what Janay got planned."

Brianna sighed heavily and rolled her eyes. Just when she was getting ready to cuss him out, he held his hand up motioning for her to be quiet while he answered his phone. She purposely sucked her teeth out loud.

"What up Ma?" He gave Brianna a look that said *don't fuck with me*. "I'll be there in a few . . . I had to see some people . . . I know this is supposed to be a pleasure trip. Just be ready when I get there." Shadee ended his call with Janay.

"What about me? Where do I fit in on this pleasure trip!" Brianna's excitement of being in Atlanta was fading fast.

"Chill out B. I'ma drop you off at the hotel and get back with you later on tonight. A'ight?"

"Sha, you brought me way down here in Atlanta to stuff me into some hotel? I don't think so! You got me twisted."

"You wanted me to send for you, so I did. Now listen at you, got the nerve to be complaining." He held out a stack of bills for her. "Do some shopping. You said you wanted to go to Phipps Plaza, right?" She had her arms folded across her chest, looking out the window, pouting. He sat the dough in her lap. "I just *can't* please you can I?"

"Please me?" she squealed. "How can you please me? You got me playing second fiddle to some dope dealin' bitch! I only ask for a little of your time. Not much. And you—"

Shadee cut her off. "B, you asked me to fuckin' send for yo ass. Now you sittin' here wildin' out like I did something to you . . ."

"Like I was saying before I was rudely interrupted. You got the audacity to say I'm never happy. Why in the hell should I be? All you do is use me to fuck and stash your shit at my house. If it wasn't for that I'd never see your black ass. You got me fucked up Shadee! I'm sick of this bullshit. All these fuckin' games you playin'. . . . Damn it, Sha!" she screamed as the Suburban came to a screeching halt, the jerking almost snapping her neck.

The valet for the Best Western opened the passenger door. "Do you need help with your luggage?"

Brianna turned towards Shadee, mouth hanging open. "Best Western?" She yelled out in a rage. "You know that I only stay at the Ritz Carlton!"

"That's where me and Janay are staying. You can't stay there. What, you want me to invite you in our fuckin' room?"

"Nigga this is a free country. I can stay wherever the fuck I wanna stay. I can't believe you gonna put me up in some god-damned Best Western! Fuck that! Move outta my way!" she yelled at the valet as she jumped out of the Suburban.

"I see that you didn't leave the money!" he yelled after her. "Bitch," he mumbled as he pulled off, picking up his cell phone and hitting the speed dial button.

"What's crackin'?" Jo Jo answered.

"Change of plans. I want this bitch to suffer. That job is off. Ya'll can chill, do whatever."

"Nigga what happened?"

"Man, that hoe got me so mad, if I didn't drop her off at the first hotel I saw I would have smoked her myself, in broad fuckin' daylight. But it's all good. She got away today. But I'm going to go with my original plan. It will be slower but at least I can watch the hoe suffer." He hung up.

Jo Jo burst out laughing. "Raney man, you ain't gonna believe this shit. I knew he couldn't do it."

"What's up?" Teraney wanted to know.

"Sha called it off. We had the perfect murder planned and this nigga calls it off!" Jo Jo still couldn't believe it.

"Man you kiddin', right? He got me traveling way across the world for shit? What he say?" Teraney's voice boomed over the radio.

"He said he wants her to suffer. So fuck it! That's on him. We down here, might as well go hit the strip joints."

"Now that sounds like a plan."

10

SHAN AND FOREVER

Shan had successfully completed three weeks of training and this was her first week on the job. She was nervous being around so many men. Men of all shapes, sizes, and colors. A mixture of murderers, drug dealers, drug users, child abusers, molesters, bank robbers, to name a few. Some of the inmates appeared to be very timid, mild-mannered, and innocent like they didn't belong in a prison surrounded by barbed wire.

In training they would place an image on the projector of a timid-looking man with glasses hanging off the tip of his nose, wearing a suit, and say, "Do you see how innocent and harmless he looks?" All of the trainees would nod yes. Then the trainer would continue. "Now look at his jacket, his criminal record." The jacket would read, armed robbery, rapist, assault with a deadly weapon.

"Excuse me ma'am." Forever peeked his head into Shan's office. "I'm reporting for duty. I'm Thompson." Shan was obviously stuck on stupid because she remained silent as she sat there staring at this perfect specimen who was an inmate. "I'll be cleaning your office and the computer classroom, right?"

"Oh. Oh? Mr. Thompson. I'm Ms. McKee." She managed to pull herself together. "Do me a favor and come see me after lunch. I'll give you your schedule and we can then get on the same page." They locked eyes. The only sounds were the distant voices down the hall.

Forever was the first to break out of the trance. "Okay, boss lady. I'll catch you after lunch." He closed the door with a sly grin on his face. Shan leaned back into her chair with a sly grin on her face as well.

"Yo, Shorty fine, ain't she?" New York Blue broke Forever out of his reverie.

"Oh, fo' sho'!"

Later on that afternoon, Forever and Shan got together and confirmed his work hours and days off. The job description sheet explained his duties. It was obvious to the both of them that sparks were flying. You could tell by the tone of their voices, Shan and her hand gestures and giggles, Forever with his outright flirting and comments.

Forever was very familiar with computer networking and programming. Shan went to college for programming but told him she hated it, that's why she switched majors. He told her that she should have hung in there because programmers get paid.

He spent the rest of the day helping her to get situated into her office, unpack and rearrange the furniture. The previous teacher, Mr. Crane, was a slob. Now the office looked as if it belonged to a woman.

"Thank you, Mr. Thompson." An exhausted Shan offered her appreciation as she plopped down into her cushiony chair. "You've made this transition very easy. I do appreciate it."

"Any time. I'm at your beck and call," the tone of his voice confirming that he meant that in more ways than one.

"See you tomorrow," they said simultaneously. Catching themselves, they both smiled.

"Where are you?" Shan yelled into the phone. "Your reception is horrible."

"I'm sitting under the hair dryer. I can hear you loud and clear. What's up? Where are you?"

"I'm home. Check this out. I think . . . do you believe in love at first sight?" Shan let out a dreamy sigh.

"Do I what?"

"You heard me. Do you believe in love at first sight?"

Brianna sucked her teeth and lifted the hair dryer up above her head. "Bitch if he's filthy rich then yes, I do believe in love at first sight. Do you hear what I'm saying? Now, is he filthy rich?"

"Brianna! If you don't get your ass back under that dryer! I'm not gonna be here with your ass all night!" Yolanda yelled.

Brianna waved her hand at her faithful hairdresser meaning for her to shut up.

"I don't know but I doubt it."

"What do you mean, you don't know? Where does he live?" Brianna probed.

If I tell you, you gotta *promise* not to judge me."

"Aawww dayum! Don't judge you? That means you gonna tell me some bullshit. What? Is he homeless?"

"See. There you go. Forget it. I can't tell you shit! You are so judgmental."

"Okay, okay. Damn! I'm just looking out for you! Who is he?"

"An inmate at the prison." Brianna was quiet this time. "Bri!" Shan yelled.

"I'm here."

"Well?"

"You didn't want me to say anything remember?"

"I want you to say *something;* I just don't want to hear anything negative. Guess what his name is?"

"What?"

"Forevvver." Shan drew his name out as if it was some chewy hot caramel dangling out of her mouth.

"Forever? Dayuum!" Brianna crossed her legs. "That sounds hot as shit."

"I know girl. And you should see him. Too bad he's in prison." Shan's words dripped with disappointment.

"Hold up." Brianna held her hand up in the air as if Shan could see it. "Let me school you. Being in prison don't mean shit. You gotta do your research. A handful of them niggas *still* gettin' money and they got money on the streets. A handful. Shit! I'll tell you what. Don't make a move without me. *We* gonna work this nigga. I'll stop by later, okay?"

"Girl, *we* ain't gonna work nobody. I got this."

"I'll be over later." *Click*. Brianna hung up while Shan was left looking at the phone.

"That bitch!"

"Checkmate, nigga! Now clean my windows!" Shan boasted. They had been sneaking and playing chess almost every day before her last class. Forever just looked at her. He was really feeling her. Their conversations were very stimulating. She was smart, genuine, fine, had an ass that he would love to squeeze and nipples that he was dying to suck. Plus, it was sweet to play a game of chess with the opposite sex. "Stop staring at me like that. Let me find out you gettin' lifted before you come to work."

"I'm lifted off of you. How you think you be winning all of the time?" he tantalized.

"Nigga, don't even try it. I'm winning because my mental is a little sharper than yours. Now clean my windows."

"Hold up. How you figure that?"

"It's obvious." Shan leaned forward resting her chin on her hands. "Chess is a mental game. Unless you are purposely allowing me to win, which I doubt very seriously, my mental is sharper than yours. Simple as that."

Brrng. Brrng. "Shan McKee," Shan sang into the phone. Forever's eyes circled her juicy lips and moved down to her nipples that were poking out of her silk blouse. He stood up while boldly keeping his eyes fixed on her nipples. Shan blushed as she watched him watch her. "Mr. Thompson." She covered the mouthpiece with her hand. "I need to take this call. Close the door on your way out."

"I got you, Ms. Mentally Sharper."

"Glad to see that real recognizes real." She smirked.

She waited until he closed the door before she let loose a huge sigh. "Big brother, I got a problem."

"I told you not to take that job. I see you gettin' caught the fuck up Shan. And don't be fuckin' with those faggot-ass niggas. All they do is use naïve-ass chicks." It was as if he was psychic.

"Oh, you sayin' your baby sis is naïve now? You about to get cussed out!"

"I'm just trying to tell you, don't fuck around and get caught up in no shit," he threatened.

"That's all you called me for?" Shan lashed out.

"I called to check on my baby sister. I know I can do that. But I'ma let you get back to your little job. I love you anyway."

"Sure," Shan dryly replied.

"What? You don't think your big brother loves you?"

"Bye Peanut."

Shan hung up on him and immediately dialed Brianna.

"Hello." Brianna sounded like she was in the tub.

"What's up, girl?"

"Shit. What's up on your end? You puttin' my plan into motion or you decided to bitch up?"

"I ain't fuckin' with you like that; I told you I'ma do me. As a matter of fact we was just in here chillin' until my big-headed brother called. He is such a blocker."

"Girl, you know how overprotective he is. That ain't gonna never change. Don't let him stop you from doing you. So what did you find out? He got dough, or what?"

"Now here you go."

"Look, if you ain't gonna do a check on the brother give me his info and I'll do it for you."

"Girl . . . Bye Brianna."

* * *

Forever and Zeke was walking the compound. "I'm in like Flynn, man. We straight. It's taking longer than I planned but I got this shit on lock!" Forever boasted with a sly grin.

"So where we at?" Zeke was getting impatient with Forever, but at the same time was confident the way Forever would make sure that all bases and their assess would be covered. Forever was the only nigga he trusted.

"You know the computer teacher, McKee?"

"Who?"

"She's my boss, man. That fine little sister with the locks." Forever looked at Zeke as if he was stupid. "Nigga don't try to act like you ain't scoped her out."

Zeke couldn't help but laugh. "She green man?"

"Green? That ain't the half of it. I know who her brother is. And he be movin' that weight. I got the shit all mapped out."

"Well let's get this shit poppin' off!" They gave each other a pound and went their separate ways.

When Forever went to check in for work, Shan was just turning the corner. He could smell her perfume as he watched the sway of her hips. She was wearing a silk burgundy pantsuit and her locks were wrapped with a burgundy scarf. She stopped at her office door and put her briefcase down and pulled out her prison key ring full of keys. As she fumbled with it Forever walked up behind her.

"You're late, Officer McKee," he said as he moved even closer. No one was in the hallway but them.

"I'm not late, you're early, Forever Thompson." She backed up into him a little.

She was just telling Brianna about him again last night. Before, she had only told her about how fine he was. But last night she spilled the beans about how they had been flirting back and forth with each other shortly after she had started work. Actually, Brianna was shocked because it was unlike Ms. Goody Two-Shoes to break the rules. She told Shan she was surprised that she was putting her job on the line. Shan told her that she was only having a little fun and now she knew where all the men were: locked up. She also told her how common it was for officers, and other staff, to be creepin' with the inmates.

When Forever felt her back up onto his dick he knew it was on. He told himself, *let the mind games begin.* He rubbed up against her and whispered, "Too bad you're not my type."

This caught Shan by surprise. As a matter of fact, she was insulted but fought to remain calm. "I can't tell." She unlocked the door and Forever pushed it open. "I need my trash dumped." She wanted to say "Nigga!" but instead said "Thompson." "And after I unlock the computer room you can clean up in there." *No, this nigga ain't tryna flip the script!* she said to herself.

Forever tried not to smile because he knew he had her right where he wanted her.

For the next few weeks he watched carefully as Shan dressed even nicer, outfits got a little tighter, perfume a little louder and was acting a little standoffish.

"Nobody likes rejection," he told Zeke.

"Man, stop the fuckin' mind games and make a move," Zeke yelled at him as he did his last set of chin-ups on the pull-up bar.

Forever finished his push-ups before responding. "I got this! Chill out. She's ready to be plucked."

"Fuck that! She's ready to be plucked but I'm ready for the bucks! Put that hoe to work. Go ahead, fuck her and get it over with! We missing out on what? Twenty-five to 30 Gs a week?"

"Man, it ain't all about the pussy. I gots to put her back up against the wall. That way I'll get the pussy handed to me on a silver platter and get her to bring my dope in. Watch how I work this hoe. You gonna crown me the king!"

Zeke could only say, "You crazy, man."

"What's going on, Thompson? You've been mighty quiet lately." Lieutenant Fargo eyed Forever suspiciously.

"What? You must want me to make some noise. What? You don't have no other excitement in your life? You need to find you some business man."

"No it's not that; I'm just surprised that you haven't been into any trouble."

Forever laughed. "Man go 'head with that. Like I said, find you some business." Forever had a gallon of wax and was pulling the buffer. He was feelin' good because he had just got off the visit with Nyla and Tameerah. "Who's gonna unlock the computer room so I can buff? You? Don't have me carrying this buffer way down there and it's locked. Y'all know how y'all do. Y'all a bunch of lazy muthafuckers!"

"No Mr. Thompson. We wouldn't do that to ya. Your boss is already down there," he said as he hit the button for the metal gate to open.

This caught Forever off-guard. "You sure man? She's never here on weekends. Am I in trouble? She said it didn't matter when I got the floor done as long as they were done by Monday morning."

The lieutenant laughed as he hunched his shoulders. "I don't know about her work schedule. But I knew trouble from you was overdue. You've been out the hole for what now, two, three months? I think you're trying to break your old record."

"Whatever man." Forever said as he dragged the buffer to the Education Department.

Forever parked the buffer and placed the bottle of wax on top of it. Instead of going to the computer room first he decided to stop at Shan's office. He tapped lightly on the door before pushing it open.

"I didn't say come in." Shan was getting ready to eat and was listening to her Floetry CD. She glanced up, "Aren't you off today? You got a pass to be down here?" She fired off at him.

Forever couldn't help but smile. He could see that she was high and had the serious munchies. "Don't yell at me because you have to work on your day off. I'm working, too, remember? Or did you forget that you have a memo posted up that says I'm sup- posed to buff this weekend? But if you want me to leave I'll leave."

"For your information I didn't forget. The door is open. I just don't want you here in my office."

"Damn. What did Forever do wrong?"

She smirked. "Forever. Did your mother name you Forever or is that some five percent Nation thing you got going on for your- self?"

Forever was still smiling. "I see you've been thinking about me." He sat down in the chair in front of her desk.

"Don't flatter yourself at my expense. Just answer the ques- tion."

"My mother gave me that name and if you act right I might let you find out if I'm living up to it or not." He was staring at her. But she was cool.

"Like I said, don't flatter yourself at my expense." She took a mouthful of her meal.

"Can I ask what are we eating?"

She looked up at him. He had on a sleeveless T-shirt and was flexing those huge muscular arms; khakis, work boots and his work gloves were in his back pocket. "We? I don't see or hear no one of French descent in this office."

"What is it? Smells good." He leaned over trying to get a better peek.

She held up a big fat shrimp. "Shrimp covered in garlic and lime juice over rice pilaf, and it is sooo good," she teased as she swallowed a shrimp.

"Is it?"

"Fo' sho." She held up another one. Soon as she did he leaned over and started sucking the shrimp and the lime juice off her fin- gers while not taking his eyes off of her. *Dayuuum,* she said to herself as her cheeks felt hot. "You know you are out of line," she said out loud.

"Who says so? It's only me and you here in this room."

"I said so."

"Well, this ain't the first time, and won't be the last time that I get out of line."

"Oh, really? When was the first time?"

"You know when it was, so stop playin' with me. Let me have another one." He looked at her plate.

She picked up another one with her fingers and he dutifully ate the shrimp and sucked on her fingers. This time a little longer. She really wanted him to suck on a little more than just her fingers. "Can I finish my dinner now?" She asked as she slowly pulled out her fingers and ran them across his pretty, juicy lips.

"You want me to leave now?"

"Yeah."

He leaned over and softly kissed her lips before going for her tongue. "Mmmm. You taste better than the garlic and lime juice." He kissed her some more. "Mmmm. You taste very good." He kissed her more hungrily this time.

She pulled away. "Let me finish my meal."

"You puttin' me out?"

"Yup. You got a floor to do and you're fuckin' up my high."

"A'ight, I'm leaving." He went to kiss her again.

"I thought I wasn't your type."

"I was just fuckin' with you."

She leaned up to kiss him but stopped in midair and then said, "Now I'm just fuckin' with you. Get the fuck outta my office!"

II

SHAN

What started out as a Saturday morning was now afternoon at the Wolfchase Galleria, for Brianna and Shan.

"Let's unload some of these bags." Brianna said to Shan as she eyed the door of Dillard's.

"Fuck unload! I'm ready to go!"

Brianna sucked her teeth. "I hate coming to the mall with you!"

"I hate coming with you, too! What else are you trying to buy?" Shan asked and looked at her with disbelief. Both of them were bogged down with bags.

"Girl, come on. I just want to hit a few more stores. Why you always gotta trip!" Brianna began walking towards the exit. "I'll buy you something. But let's drop this load."

Shan started laughing. "Hoe, you gonna have to buy me a lot to get me to come back in here. It's damn near 2:00!"

"I got you! I got you!"

"You better have me!"

When they arrived at Brianna's Lexus it began to drizzle but the sun was still shining. They stuffed all of the bags into the trunk. "I feel weird today." Shan shrugged. "Something's going down."

"Weird?"

"Yeah. You know, like something's going on but you just can't pinpoint it? And last night I had a dream about snakes, bit fat ones! They were everywhere. I was beating them with sticks but they were coming out of every hole. If I moved a rock, a big one would come slithering out. That shit was weird." Shan slammed the trunk shut.

"You don't have to slam it!"

"Girl, please! Unlock the damn door." Shan ordered.

"A'ight now. You break it. You pay for it!" Brianna said, trying to sound like a Chinese salesperson. "What do you think your dream meant?"

"I don't know. But that shit was scary. I hope it wasn't telling me that you're a snake," Shan teased.

"Whatever, hoe." Brianna started the car and drove to a corner in the rear of the mall parking lot. Shan got comfortable and pulled out the dro. "So whose paper you spending today?" Shan put fire to the blunt while she fixed her gaze on Brianna.

Tssk!" Brianna emphatically sucked her teeth. "Shadee's. It's his guilt money. He had the audacity to send for me, while he's chillin' in Atlanta with his baby's mama. Then he had the nerve to have her all up in the Ritz Carlton while dropping me off at some Best Western. I said, 'nigga, you got me twisted!' I went the fuck off!" Shan was laughing so hard she was choking. "Bitch, it ain't that funny!" snapped Brianna. "Pass the haze." She snatched the blunt out of Shan's hand before continuing. "I didn't even check into the hotel. I stuffed the dough in my bag, hailed me a cab back to the airport and was on the first flight back home."

Still laughing Shan said, "Now that's a relationship I'm still trying to figure out."

They sat and puffed while listening to K-97.1. Of course Brianna had to pick up her cell phone. She was expecting a call from Peanut. As soon as she hung up she tried to convince Shan to walk back to the mall instead of drive. "Girl, it's beautiful out and plus we'll be driving around *forever* trying to find a spot that's closer."

"Oooooh! Don't say that name." Shan put her palms over her ears.

"What exactly is your problem?" Brianna laughed. "Whose name did I say?"

"Forever hoe! You know what name."

"Bitch please! Forever is nothing but an infatuation. At least he better be." She stared down at Shan. "You can't have him, he's married, he's locked up, and you ain't trying to find out if he got any money. So why waste the pussy? Oops! My bad! I forgot. With you it's not all about the money," she cracked.

"You are so funny. Ha! Ha! Girl, just shut up. Let's go before I change my mind." Shan opened the car door. She really did not want B to know that they had been kissing. Brianna don't even give out kisses for free. And Shan knew Forever wanted to fuck her.

"A'ight Forever! You know I'm telling the truth." Brianna laughed. "You gonna get enough of giving out charity pussy."

When they stepped out of the car the sun was beaming and the drizzle had stopped.

"Ooh! It is beautiful out." Shan beamed.

"I don't know why you're just noticing, Miss Ready-To-Go-Home. Hmmp! Look who I see. Turn to your left partna, so you can see a nigga with money fo' real!"

When Shan turned to look she said, "Got damn! I knew I was feeling tensed up for some reason." She rolled her eyes at Briggen, who was wearing a Knicks jersey, black jean shorts and some crisp white-on-white Birdman sneakers. He also looked as if he had just come from the barber. Him and his boy was sitting in his truck smokin' and chillin' while Brianna and Shan was parked a few spaces down. He was patiently waiting for them to pull off or get out of the car.

"Shan baby, come here, girl."

Shan acted as if she didn't hear him.

"Girl, answer him so that I can holla at that nigga he got wit him."

"I am not in the mood to be fuckin' with him B. He ain't shit and you know that. So come on. Let's roll." Brianna was stalling, pretending to look for something in the trunk. "Come on, Brianna. Stop playing. He ain't nothin' but trouble."

"Trouble? He can't be no more trouble than Mr. Forever. Look at him! All I see is pussy in his eyes! How much trouble is that? You said he got tha bomb dick." That caused Shan to crack a smile.

"You are so ignorant. You can't even see his eyes from here, hoe!" Before she could say another word he was standing behind her, wrapping his arms around her waist.

"Woo. This right here is Shan. I told you about her."

"The lil' mama who raped you then put you out?" Woo teased.

"Yeah. This is her." Then he looked at Brianna. "Brianna this is my boy, Woo. Woo, this is Brianna." He nodded to Woo. Brianna was flashing her Ms. America smile. She was immediately in his face asking him where he was from and getting her mack on.

"How come you told him that?" Shan was embarrassed.

Briggen was slowly steering Shan toward his truck, which was gleaming like it just came from getting detailed. "I thought that was you." He ignored her question.

"I'm on my way to the mall, so let me go. Why are we walking towards your ride? And what? You're following me now?"

"You tryna call me a stalker?"

"What's up Calvin? What do you want? I suggest you get back home to your Stepford Wives."

"Ha. Ha. Cute. I didn't forget that cute little stunt you pulled that night. And why are you always ignoring me?"

"You're ignoring me. I just asked you a question! And why do you always answer me with a question?" Shan couldn't even front, she still had some feelings for him.

"Why do we always have to fight? Instead, why can't we make love?"

"Because you don't got it like that! Bri let's go!" she yelled and tried to turn them around.

Briggen wouldn't let her go and kept steering her towards his truck. "Where do you think you're trying to go? I want to talk to you."

"About what?"

"You know about what. How you keep standing me up, ignoring me; you know what's up. You won't return my calls or nothing. Why you gotta be so hard on a nigga?"

"And you still can't take a hint. How many times do I need to spell it out for you?" she said with much sarcasm and attitude.

"You're right. Spell it out. You know I don't take hints." He opened the back door.

"I don't know why you're opening the door, I'm not gettin' in." When Briggen picked her up she started screaming and laughing. "Boy, stop playing!" She placed her feet firmly on the edge of the seat, trying to stop him. She screamed as he lifted her higher and slid her across the seat. He climbed in and shut the door. "What do you want?" He felt for his keys, leaned up, started the engine and turned on the air. "What do you want Briggen?"

"I want to talk to you!"

"About what?"

"Me and you. Making things right."

"I told you before. You fucked up the first time. Plus you got a little too much goin' on for me. Let's just be friends and leave it at that."

"Whatever happened to second chances?"

"I told you before; with me you only get one chance. I don't know why you refuse to acknowledge that. Now let me out. I'm ready to go finish gettin' my shop on, Playboy. How much money you got on you?" Shan joked.

"A lot and you can have it all if you give me some time."

"Yeah, right. I've given up my time. We've been sitting here for ten minutes."

"Not that kind of time. I want some of dis pussy. Do me like you did the last time. Let me give you some head, then put me outta my own truck. I won't even be mad. That's how bad I want to taste some of dis pussy."

Shan laughed. "Some pussy? What? Sitting right here in the

backseat in the parking lot? Nigga, please! You ain't my man. Only my man would have it like that."

"I'm tryna be your man but you won't let me."

"Cut the bullshit! Like I said, you had your chance Playboy. But we are not going to even waste our time arguing about that." She went to grab the door but he grabbed her hands.

"What about the feelings you had for me? You know you still got some so don't front!"

"Yeah. You said the key word: HAD! I've moved on and it's your loss." She grabbed the car door handle, pushed it open and got out. Briggen was right behind her. "Now give me some cash." She turned around and held out her hand. "I want to buy something."

He grabbed her hand and pulled her close. "And I want some pussy," he ordered as he was squeezing her ass and sucking on her neck. "I saw all of them bags. You already bought a whole lotta sumthin'!"

"Briggen, stop it! Do not put any hickeys on my neck!"

He held her even closer. "Why? I'ma piss your man off? Well, give me a kiss and maybe I'll think about letting you go."

"I don't think so!"

His lips went to the other side of her neck. "Ouch! Briggen, stop! Let me go!"

"Now I want a kiss and a hug!"

She stood on her tiptoes and gave him a quick peck on the lips. "You are so ignorant."

"Oh, hell naw baby. Don't tease me. You gonna have to come wit it!"

"Why you gotta play with me Briggen?" She really did like him.

"Keep stalling and I'll be taking me some of this pussy. Now come on and give me a kiss." Shan gave a peck on the lips and then another one. Briggen held onto them lips, grabbed that tongue, and they didn't come up for air until her pussy was throbbing.

When Briggen sensed how turned on she was he asked, "You sure you don't want to give a nigga some of dis pussy?"

"Nigga please, I'm not that turned on."

"Yes you are."

"Well you already know all of your privileges have been cut off." They kissed again and couldn't help but hear the bass knockin' in the background.

"Can I come over later?"

Shan was melting in his arms. "Call me."

The Low Rider stopped and the windows rolled down. Briggen heard Woo yell, "Cover up, Brig! Cover up! Dive down!" as Woo began firing into the Low Rider.

Pop! Pop! Pop! Pop! Pop! The gunfire rang from out of the Low Rider. "What's up now, motherfucker?" Somebody yelled. Then there was laughter.

"Fuck?" Briggen spat as he felt burning sensations.

Shan started screaming when she saw the first squirt of blood and couldn't make herself stop. The world appeared to be moving in slow motion as she fell backwards with Briggen's heavy, twitching body pressed to hers. Blood was oozing out of the corner of his mouth and he was trembling. Shan knew she was screaming but couldn't hear a thing.

The tires squealed as the Low Rider took off.

Woo obviously hit a target because there was blood splattered all over the side window. Brianna and Woo ran over. "Shan! Shan! Oh, my God, Shan!" B was mumbling. "Oh, God, Shan, are you all right? I'm sorry. I should have taken you home when you wanted to leave. I'm sorry. Please, God, let her be all right."

"Fuck!" Woo stomped. "You hit man! You hit!"

"Go now," Briggen was trying to tell Shan. "Go!"

Shan squirmed out from underneath him. Brianna grabbed her arm. "Come on, Shan! Come on! Let's go! Damn! Let's go! We gotta get outta here!" She was pulling Shan, who was staring at Briggen. "C'mon girl! Let's fuckin' get outta here!"

12

SHADEE

"Hello."

"Crystal, it's me. Where's your sister? What's up with her and that nigga who drives the Beamer? I go—"

Crystal cut him off. "Hold on Sha, let me go to another phone."

Shadee heard her door slam and then Crystal fumbling with the phone. "Crystal what the fuck is goin' on? She leaves this message, crying and shit, talkin' bout come and get her. But she doesn't say where the fuck she is!"

"Sha, shit has been crazy!" Crystal blurts out and then starts crying. "Janay said they was gonna kill her. She took over Big Choppa's business; they're jealous and she didn't want nobody to get hurt. But she had to do what she had to do. She scared to leave. She said she didn't plan on taking over his spot, it just fell into her lap . . . she . . . Daddy's chemo, the doctors, I don't . . ."

"Girl slow the fuck down! You ain't making any sense. Where is she?" Sha screamed into the phone.

"Getwell Gardens."

"Getwell Gardens? Why the fuck is she down there?"

"That's her spot. I don't know what building. I just know the building's in the back, Big Choppa's newest spot."

Shadee hung up on Crystal and dialed Kay-Gee's celly.

"What's good Sha?" Kay-Gee's loud mouth yelled.

"Yo, sumthin's up. Get your tools and the crew. Meet me at the Getwell Gardens. But don't do shit, just wait for me."

Shadee hung up and dialed Born.

"What up Unc?"

"I'm around the corner. I need my tools. Where you at?"

"I'm on the block but sounds like we about to go to war. So that's what's up?"

"We'll see. Meet me at your crib in fifteen."

Shadee was already sitting in front of Born's apartment building on Riverside Drive when him and Teraney pulled up. Born jumped out and ran over to Shadee who was on his phone. No one spoke until they got upstairs to his apartment.

Teraney couldn't contain himself. "What's happenin' Sha? Who we got beef wit?" Teraney was always trigger happy and always ready for drama.

"Everybody man. How come nobody knows about the competition? Like whose servin' Big Choppa's peeps? Why we ain't on it? What! Y'all niggas ain't hungry no more?" Shadee was yelling as he went to the back to get the guns. "Y'all niggas slippin'!"

"Ain't nobody slippin'. You always outta town man. I'm on it. Jeff K and Biz took over."

"That ain't what I'm hearin'."

"Those are your girl's peeps. You said to let 'em ride for now. Am I right?" Born was looking at Shadee hoping that that's what Shadee had said. Born was not one to hold his tongue.

"Strap up nigga!" Shadee threw two glocks at him.

"What's happenin' yo?" Teraney was strapping up as well as he joined them in the back.

"We're gettin' ready to find out."

They jumped in Born's ride and headed for the projects. They circled around first to see what was up. Everything seemed to be ghetto as usual. Kids were still out playing even though it was dark. Niggas was hangin' on the corner slangin', hoes were on the stroll, the crack fiends were prowling and the teens were chillin', smokin' blunts, pumpin' the music of Three 6 Mafia. As soon as they parked Kay-Gee pulled up next to them. Shadee rolled down the passenger window.

"Yo! What's poppin' Sha?" Kay-Gee wanted to know.

"I really don't know but we got to go in expectin' a war. Janay done got herself into something man. Foreal, Foreal; I'm not sure what the fuck is the story. I do know one thing though. Seems like between all of us mutherfuckers, we would know what the fuck is going on in our own backyard. Shit's gonna have to change. And if this bitch been slingin' behind my back I'ma put my foot in her ass!"

Kay-Gee nodded yeah, seeing that his man was pissed off. "A'ight man, I heard you. We ready. I'ma leave Jo Jo here with the whips. The rest of us, we ready to roll wit you. Let's do it!" They left all of the vehicles parked in the middle of the street with big ass Jo Jo.

Teraney spotted one of his boys who use to be large on the block, but was now smoked out. "What up Spontaine? Let me holla at you!" Teraney was trying hard to wipe the look of disgust off his face. Spontaine was pitch black and ashy. His hair was matted to his head and he was wearing a dirty cable uniform. His hustle was going around hookin' up peeps' cable for a rock.

"Raney, what's good? You got all the channels man? Pay Per View? The works?" Spontaine wasted no time going into his sales pitch. "If not, you know I'm yo man. I can hook you up today. You still my nigga. I'm just doin' a little sumthin' sumthin' until I get back on my feet."

"I hear you man." Teraney pulled out ten dollars. "Which apartment is the whole show runnin' from?"

Spontaine snatched the ten-dollar bill. "Man, its been dry and quiet for the last coupla days. Nobody ain't been runnin' shit!

That bitch that's up there, I don't know what's up with her. She rules with an iron fist. Big Choppa be lookin' out. We just been watching and waitin'; most fiends been coppin' elsewhere, you know how that go." He pointed to the buildings in the back. "Foreal, Foreal—I don't think nobody's back there. There has been no movement except for a few hoes turning tricks, but nobody's answerin' the door. The whole building is theirs. Big Choppa got it on lock."

Teraney pulled out another ten. "Yeah, well spread the word that the bitch and everybody relocated. A'ight?"

"I got you man. Can I get a rock instead of the ten?"

"Nigga, you just said you tryna get yourself together." Teraney put the ten back in his pocket and turned to walk away.

"Yo wait! A'ight, man. Gimme tha ten. You got some work for me? I need to come up."

"I'll get back at you." And he turned to Shadee. "Sha!" He pointed behind him. "That's the spot. Top floor. They got the whole building. Word is some bitch been runnin' shit but it's been quiet for the last two days. Damn man. You really think that's Janay?" Teraney didn't know whether to be shocked or impressed. He knew that Big Choppa was her pops. He also heard rumors that he taught both of his daughters every detail of the "Game." And word on the street was, whenever Big Choppa would get sick, Janay was the one to hold it down for him. She would oversee the smooth running of his entire operation. Now it appeared to be déjà vu. The most impressive rumor was she caught her first body before her eighteenth birthday. To Teraney, that was really gangsta, especially for a female.

"Yeah man. It's her." They all marched with Shadee to the spot where she was supposed to be. They definitely looked like they were on a mission.

When the fiends spotted Born they all rushed over to see if he needed something.

"Move the fuck outta my way!" he yelled, pushing the fiend

closest to him, causing him to fall on his back right on top of some dog shit.

"Aw, dayuum!" somebody yelled and everybody started laughing.

"Oh shit! I think them niggas run New Chicago." A young fifteen-year-old soldier said.

"What they doin' out here?" his partna asked.

"Naw." CK, a kid whose oldest brother worked for Big Choppa, interrupted. "Those are Big Choppa's peeps. That bitch in there is getting ready to get her brains blown out."

"They ain't Big Choppa's peeps!" the young soldier challenged. I told ya them niggas run New Chicago. They probably gettin' ready to take over!" New Chicago was a Memphis hood and huge money-making spot.

Everyone was speculating and curious as to what was happening as Shadee and his crew marched through the crowd looking as if they were about to blow something up. Shadee pushed the hall door open and already had his glock cocked. The building reeked of crack, weed, beer, wine, and urine all mixed together. It was a building that belonged to the fiends. All of the apartments were condemned and were used only to get high and turn tricks.

Shadee banged on the steel door. "Goddamn! What is this, Fort Knox? Janay!"

Plop! Plop! Everyone turned behind them and was aiming. "Chill out!" Teraney said.

"Chill out? How the fuck we gonna chill and you shootin'!" Shadee looked at Teraney as if he was crazy.

"It was a rat, dawg. You know I hate them sons a bitches."

All they heard was groans and mumbles as everybody wanted to shoot Teraney personally.

Shadee had his ear to the door. "Damn yo. It sounds like I hear some ticking."

"This shit could be booby trapped Unc!" Born's eyes was big as saucers.

"Hell, yeah," Kay-Gee chimed in.

"Well, we bout to find out, niggas." He banged some more. "Janay! You in there?" he yelled out as he banged harder.

The slot where the drugs were passed through opened and then closed. When the door opened Shadee went in first with his gun cocked. "Shadee, put the guns away. I'm the only one here." She stood behind the door wearing blue shorts and a white top. Her sneakers were untied, hair up in a ponytail and the tears were falling down her cheeks. She went to close the door but Born and Teraney stepped through.

"Whoa, girl! You gonna kill a nigga with that steel door," Born said. Behind him was Slim and Kay-Gee.

"Did you have to bring the army with you?" she wanted to know, looking at Shadee.

"I didn't know what to bring. How the fuck I was supposed to know?"

"Put the guns up y'all," Janay scolded.

"What the fuck is goin' on Janay? And what is that smell? I hope it's not what I think it is," Shadee said.

"What's going on? What about, how are you baby? I miss you. I've been busy but I'ma make it up to you. Why I gotta go through drama to get your attention? Where have you been Sha? You better believe if I had someone else to call I would not have called you!" She rattled off.

Shadee was standing in the middle of the floor looking around and ignoring her outburst while kinda surprised and shocked at what he saw. There was a long picnic table against the wall. It was covered with bags of all sizes of crack, powder, and weed. On the kitchen table there were two duffel bags.

"Don't nobody touch shit!" he yelled. "Janay stop bitchin' for a minute and bag up all that shit on the table." He went over to the duffel bags and just as he thought, they were filled with money. He grabbed both of those.

"Yo Unc! Come here!" Born yelled from the back.

"Don't touch shit!" he yelled again, looking around at the others. He went down the hall to where Born was. Born stepped out of the room with a handkerchief around his nose and mouth. Shadee stepped in the room. "Oh damn!" He yelled and jumped back into the hallway. His eyes began to water. He pulled his jersey up over his nose and mouth and went back inside to look at the three dead bodies lying on the floor.

"Damn Janay," he mumbled.

13

BRIANNA

"Is he dead? Is he dead?" Was all Shan could get out. "Brianna, did they kill him?" She was screaming.

"Shan, I was never so fuckin' scared in all my life. You worrying about him? If that would have been you, I swear I don't know what I would have done. You are like my shadow." Brianna's hands was trembling as she tried to keep them steady on the steering wheel.

"So he is dead? Brianna I should have done something! Is he dead?"

"I don't know Shan."

"Then why are you so scared and shaking?"

"Never saw nobody get shot before. Not up close. And at first I thought you was hit. You're the only family I got who loves me for me. You don't judge me. The thought of you not being here for me spooked the shit outta me. I need to get myself together. That was a wake up call. That was too scary for me."

Shan began to cry harder. "He's dead. I should have kept him in the truck. Oh, God, Brianna!"

"Shan! Pull yourself together!" She had been trying to block out Shan's screaming and crying, during the entire ride home. "Let me get you inside," Brianna said as she pulled up in front of her building. She jumped out, then took Shan inside. She immediately peeled the bloody clothes off of Shan's trembling body.

"You know I have to get rid of these don't you?" Shan nodded her head yes. Brianna started the shower and noticed that Shan was in a daze. "Shan! Shan!" She grabbed both shoulders and squeezed them tight. "Get in the shower. You can do that, right?" *Oh, my God!* Brianna said to herself. "C'mon." She guided Shan into the warm water and closed the curtain. "I'll be right back." She gathered up the blood-soaked clothes, put them into a trash bag and put them into the Dumpster. She then ran back inside and straight to the bathroom, only to find Shan in the same spot that she left her. She grabbed her lavender body wash and began lathering up Shan's body; she felt as if she was bathing a child. After her entire body was lathered up she turned Shan around in circles so that she could rinse her off. She turned the water off, grabbed a towel and dried her off. After giving her some pajamas she got her comfortable and tucked her under the covers. "I'll be right back." Brianna ran outside and unloaded all of their shopping bags. When she came back inside and checked on Shan, she was still crying.

"Bri, get me something for my head. It's killing me."

"It should be. You've been crying nonstop in a damn zombie trance. Let me see what I've got. I should have something." Brianna went to her bathroom and checked her medicine cabinet.

When she came back she had one pill and a glass of water. "What is this? I just want some Tylenol or something. Not no damn psyche meds!" Shan said, knowing how Brianna was.

"Girl, please. Do you want your headache to stop or what? Plus, this will put you to sleep for an hour or two. It's not gonna kill you."

"Yeah. Psyche meds, just as I thought." Shan said but swallowed the pill anyway.

"Don't let me sleep long." She turned over and then cried, "B, they shot him. One of those bullets could have hit me. He fell right on top of me. Was he dead B?"

"I don't know. I mean, I don't think so. Shan please try to relax and get some sleep. I'll see if I can find something out." She ran her hands through Shan's hair and rocked her to sleep. Then she got up and turned out the light.

Brianna tried calling Woo but kept getting his voice mail. She put down her cell phone to answer the house phone.

"Hello."

"Hey. What you doing? I need to swing by." It was Shadee.

"I got company right now. But I'm glad you called."

"You got a nigga over but you're glad I called? Girl you full of shit! You know that, right?"

"A nigga? It's my girl Shan. You can come over. I gotta talk to you about something."

"Shan, huh? A'ight. I'm on my way."

As soon as she hung up, the phone rang again. "Collect call from Skye at the Wayne County Jail. Will you accept?" Bri was caught off-guard and her heart was jammed in her throat. *Oh, shit! The county jail?* She thought to herself.

"Skye?"

"Yes. Will you accept the call, ma'am?"

"Uh, um, yes, yes, I will."

"Go ahead, sir."

"Yo Brianna! You got me fucked up!" his voice screamed through.

"Skye? Where are you?"

"In fuckin' Detroit waitin' for my boy to post my bail. You better hope my man is here before our prints come back! Your man Peanut that you put me up on? That nigga was hot as fuck! Then on top of that, you didn't tell us he's into all that gangbangin' shit. He been getting his ass beat. I even heard that they busted him a new asshole. He's fucked being that he's way down here in enemy territory."

"How y'all get way in Detroit?"

"Don't worry about that. You need to worry about what's

gonna happen if I don't get out before my prints come back. If my boy don't come through you better find a way to get down here."

"What about who you had with you when you got locked up? Was it a total loss? What about Peanut? Can't y'all bail him out too?" Brianna was having trouble breathing. It was taking everything within her to not freak out.

"Bitch, what you been smokin'? How we gonna rob the nigga then get him out of jail? That defeats the purpose! Don't go catching feelings for him now. You didn't have no feelins when you put me on him."

"Skye, I don't want nothing out the deal, just get him out. That's my girl's brother."

"You wasn't getting shit no way! The whole deal went bust. But I'll see what I can do as far as lookin' out for him. Dude in a fucked up situation."

"Don't try. Do something Skye! The whole deal ain't go bust because your boy is out and he's gettin' you out. Nigga, don't try to play me. A deal's a deal."

"Trick, I said I'll see what I can do." *Click.*

Brianna grabbed a pillow off the sofa, put it to her face and went to bawling like the rotten low-down bitch she was. She stayed in that position for the next twenty minutes, all the way until Shadee came knocking on the door.

When he stepped inside he looked at Brianna in tears and immediately regretted that he stopped by. He was not in the mood for any female drama. And he damned sure didn't want to hear about that Atlanta bullshit. Plus, he had absolutely no more love for her. He went straight to the back to where his safe was and deposited some dope and cash.

"Where's your girl?"

"She's asleep in my bed." She looked up at him. "Sha, I don't know what I'ma do. I really fucked up this time. Oh, God, I fucked up. Sha, I don't know what to do." And she burst out crying once again.

Shadee sat on the sofa across from her, stretched out his long legs and placed his hands behind his head. *Yeah, bitch, shed them fucking tears. 'Cause what I got for your bitch ass, you ain't gonna like.* He thought to himself.

"Why are you looking at me like that?" She jumped up and ran into the bathroom.

"Looking at you like what?" he hollered after her.

Brianna dried her face, grabbed some tissue and peeked in on Shan, who was still sleeping. She came back into the living room and sat down next to Shadee.

"Sha, I really fucked up this time. My shit has finally caught up with me. I don't knock tha next man's hustle. So why do thugs and bitches always gotta knock mines?" She grabbed an ashtray, pulled out a joint, and lit it with trembling hands. "Sha," B continued, "do you know what my hustle is?" She passed him the joint and watched wide-eyed as he took a long pull.

When Sha finished coughing he said, "Yeah, I know what's up."

"You do?" She looked surprised.

"Brianna that's your problem. You think everybody is stupid." He glared at her with contempt. "You ain't as game tight as you think you are."

She buried her face in her hands and was silent for a few minutes. "Why do you still fuck with me Sha?"

He smiled. "Like you said, 'don't knock tha next man's hustle.' Plus, who am I to judge?"

"But Sha, I really, really . . . my hustle is getting knocked right now. I fucked up big time!"

"If you play B, you gotta be ready to pay. That's part of the game."

"I know. But I didn't mean for my girl's brother to pay." She blew her nose. "This nigga Skye I hooked up with, I put him on my girl's brother. Well, things got botched somehow, at least that's what he told me and they are locked up in Detroit. But that's not all. It gets even more fucked up." She blew her nose again. "Peanut is a gangbanger and Detroit is enemy territory. They're beating him up and raping him," she bawled and blew her nose again. "And they're probably gonna kill him Sha, and it's all my fault!" She burst out crying again. "Shan is my family Sha. I set her brother up. I did shit to a lot of niggas. But how low did I have to go? My best, shit, my only friend! And on top of that, I fucked one of the only niggas that really got love for me and is not out to use me . . . You, Sha," she mumbled.

"Come again," Sha said, knowing damn well what she was getting at, but couldn't believe that she was actually going to confess. He pulled out his own blunt.

"I fucked you Sha." Brianna, for some reason, felt the need to confess. "I set you up before Sha. Hook and Rob was most likely with him. I owed Hook and I knew you was coming to get something small. I know you always put a little something aside for the robbers." She blew her nose. "So I knew it was no big deal. But then I saw you with them stitches in your head . . . Sha, I am so sorry. You could have gotten killed. I just thought that you would give them what you had on you. I was scared to tell you Sha. I'm so sorry. If I could take it back, I would." She was now crying so hard he thought she was gonna throw up.

For the next ten minutes Sha smoked on his blunt as Brianna cried. The only thing he was thinking about was implementing his plan on paying this bitch back.

"Sha."

He looked at her. "What's up?" It was taking all of his manpower to not put both hands around her neck and squeeze until her eyeballs popped outta their sockets.

"I'm sorry."

"I ain't sweatin' it. I just have to charge it to the game."

Brianna looked at him and could feel that that's what his mouth was saying but she knew that he was disappointed in her.

"Fuck!" she said out loud.

Sha stood up to leave.

"What am I gonna do?" she pleaded with him. "Peanut is stuck in jail. I don't know if he got somebody to bail him out or not. Shan's over here. I know he's been calling her house. We've been at the mall all day." Briggen getting shot was the last thing on her mind. "If I get him out myself, he's gonna know I set him up. If I don't get him out, that's not fair to him or Shan. What do you think I should do?"

"Get who out? And I know you ain't sheddin' them kind of tears for Briggen." Shan was standing in the living room with Brianna's robe on. "Hoe, what have you gotten yourself into now?"

14

FOREVER

Forever smiled as he went to meet Nyla as she rushed through the visiting room doors and jumped into his arms.

"Babee!" she squealed as she kissed him on the lips. "Thank you for the roses!" She gave him another big kiss. "Thank you for the minivan." She kissed him again. "I love you so much." *Kiss.* I heard this car horn beeping in the driveway; I was like, who in the world is that! It was almost 11:00. Babee, why didn't you tell me?"

Nyla was talking a mile a minute she was that excited. Today was her birthday and she took off from work to come visit Forever. She was hoping to get a minivan to accommodate her new floral arrangements/party favorites business. What had started as a hobby had blossomed into a part-time business.

"As long as you're happy, you know I'm happy. Happy Birthday baby." It was his turn to take a few kisses. "Where's my other baby?" Forever wanted to know.

"In school where she belongs. This is my day."

"She's gonna whip your ass if she finds out you came to see her daddy without her."

"She is, ain't she? That girl is something else."

"So are you. She's just like her momma."

"You got some picture tickets, right?"

"Of course. It's my baby's birthday and look at you." He spun her around. "Lookin' all cute, wearing my 'Forever make me cum' skirt. You know I like that shit." He pulled her close.

"You better like it! I know you got my freak letter last night. Didn't you?" She was grinning.

"Yeah I got it." He kissed her on the lips.

"And?"

"It was a'ight."

"A'ight? Nigga please! Don't make me hurt you."

Forever laughed. "It was good."

"Good huh?"

"Mmm-mmm."

"Well? Tell me what you liked the best. Tell me something!"

"Or what?"

"Stop playing Forever." She pulled away from him.

"A'ight. A'ight. Come here!" He pulled her back. "Let's see. Where should I start? With all them different positions? Those were hot! Or you giving me a full body hot oil massage? I liked that. Or us bustin' nuts at the same time? Hmmm?" He kissed her on the cheek. "Or, should I start with you licking the whip cream off my dick and swallowing my cum? Or how you really got creative and described how you want me to slurp a Twix outta your pussy?" Nyla couldn't help but laugh. "So, where do you want me to start?"

"I *was* pretty creative wasn't I? Just the thought of that Twix makes my pussy hot," she whispered in his ear as she slid her hand down and squeezed his dick. "Give your wife another kiss." She ran her hand up and down his dick while he sucked on her tongue.

"Yo! Break that shit up! This ain't the Radisson!" Zeke yelled.

Nyla ended the kiss and looked back at Zeke. "Why you tryna block?"

"And I love you too, Cousin. Now come here!" She broke away from Forever and met Zeke halfway. Zeke gave her a big bear hug. "Happy Birthday Cousin! How old did you say you were?" he teased.

"I didn't. Nigga how you gonna send me a birthday card with no money in it?" She punched him in the arm.

"Ow!" he yelled. "Hey, officer!" he joked. "Now you know I got you baby cousin. Your birthday ain't over yet!"

"You better have me or else your ass is cut off!" she threatened.

"Where's my other baby cousin?"

"In school where she belongs. Like I told her father, this is my day." The two females who were watching them caught Nyla's attention.

"I ain't mad at you." Zeke peepin' out what had her attention said, "Let me introduce you to Crystal and Danisha."

"Crystal *and* Danisha," she repeated and he laughed. "Zeke, how many hoes do you have? Let me find out you pimpin' behind bars!"

"Cousin, I already told you. Hoes is like pants to me. Depending on my mood that's what I'll go and get into."

"That's really pimpish of you." Nyla snapped back. "Especially since you're in prison. Y'all are only allowed five pairs of pants, right?"

That got a laugh outta Zeke. "Naw, Foreal, Foreal, this is business."

"Mixed with pleasure, I'm sure. So I guess the other hoe pulled Forever out." Nyla slid in.

"Yo, Forever! Get your woman dawg." Zeke gave her another hug then went back and sat between Crystal and Danisha.

When Forever took Nyla by the hand she sarcastically asked, "Where are we gonna sit?"

"I want you to sit over here for two minutes, and I'll be right with you."

"What? You gotta tell your hoe good-bye?"

"That hoe is the force behind that brand new minivan parked in your driveway," Forever snapped and walked away.

He was back in two minutes just as he had said. He sat in front of her and pulled her to the edge of the seat. She had an attitude, refusing to look at him and kept both arms and legs crossed.

"You ain't stoppin' nothin'," Forever said as he ran his hand over her calf, up the back of her thigh, then under it and then plunging two fingers into her pussy.

"Foreeever," she moaned.

"What?" He was moving his fingers in and out as he leaned over and kissed her lips. "I know you gonna let a nigga handle his business right?"

"Daddy, that feels good." She kissed him on the lips.

"Answer me Nyla. You gonna let a nigga handle his business, right?"

"Yes."

"A'ight then. We gonna start this visit all over again."

After the visit, Forever ended up in the Education Department mopping the floors when he looked up and saw Shan coming down the hall. Her eyes were puffy; she was causally dressed and didn't appear to be her normal vibrant self. She went straight into her office without even acknowledging him. After he finished mopping he put away all of the supplies and went to check in. He knocked on the door and then pushed it open.

"Do you need anything before I go back to my unit?"

She looked up at him. "Do you mind washing out that coffee-pot and making some more? Please?"

"Not a problem." Forever grabbed the pot and scrubbing pad. When he came back she was just hanging up the phone and tears were flowing down her cheeks. He grabbed the box of tissues, passed it to her, then went back to making the coffee. He glanced over at her.

"Yo Ma. You wanna talk about it?" She shook her head no. "Why?"

"Thanks for making my coffee. You can go now." She blew her nose.

"Why don't you want to talk about it?"

"Why should I? It's none of your business."

"I could be of some help. You never know."

"Yeah, right."

"Try me. You'll never know unless you do."

She sucked her teeth and rolled her eyes.

"Try me," he urged. He kept staring at her until she gave in.

"Okay, Mr. Big Shot around the tier. I need $35,000, like yesterday." She leaned back into her chair, folded her arms across her chest and glared at him.

Why do women always fold their arms across their chest when they're pissed? he asked himself.

"What? Cat got your tongue, Mr. Big Shot?" She smirked as she watched him close the door and then pour her a cup of coffee.

"How much sugar you want in this?"

"It doesn't matter. So? What's up?"

"You want some cream?"

"It doesn't matter."

"A'ight. I'll make it like me, brown and sweet." He winked at her, then stirred the coffee, handed her the cup and sat down in one of the chairs in front of her desk.

"Thanks. You can go now."

"I thought you needed some assistance like yesterday?"

"Yeah, I do and nothing has changed in the last two minutes."

"We can help each other out."

"Meaning?"

"You need the cash and I need some packages delivered, like yesterday. So like I said, we can help each other out."

"Forever, don't play with me. This is no fuckin' joke."

"Do I look like I'm playing?" They glared at each other for a few minutes.

She turned on the radio. "You got my attention."

Forever grabbed a sheet of paper and a pencil. "I'ma give you a name and number. Call him and tell him you're calling for Silk. He'll arrange to meet you and give you a package. Thursday night you got between 8:30 and 9:15 to drop it in the middle garbage can in the employee parking lot."

"That's it? Will that work?" This seemed too easy for Shan.

"Depends on you. Eight-thirty, no later than 9:15. Can you handle that?"

She stared at him. "Are you a cop?"

"No. Are you?" he asked, already knowing the answer. He'd done thorough research on her before contacting his boy Skye.

"No. Can I get the money on Thursday when the package is dropped off?"

"The agreement is *packages* dropped off. Not package." He was watching her closely. "Are you in, or what?"

"I'm in but I told you I need the money like yesterday."

"I'll see what I can do. A'ight?"

"A'ight."

Forever got up to leave. When he got to the door he said, "And for the record, I'm not the big shot on the tier. I'm the HNIC of the whole prison." He winked at her, turned and left out. "Damn. Shit played into my hands better than I thought. And I don't even have to fuck her. I owe my man Skye big time for this one!"

15

PEANUT AND SHAN

"Hey, Youngblood," ole man Smoke said to Peanut.

"What's up, OG?" Peanut raised up on his elbows. He had been sleeping with one eye open and one eye closed since they took him into custody. Ex-Blood or not, he still was in Crip territory. He was surrounded. Once he gave the Blood handshake to a homie being discharged it spread like wildfire. Not even an hour later he had his first altercation, where only words were exchanged. The following morning three Crips asked him what set he represented. He told them that he didn't get down like that no more and walked away. At lunchtime as he turned the corner heading for the stairs, he was slashed across his back.

"Aww, fuck!" he yelled as the burning sensation hit him. He turned around and saw two blue bandannas turn the corner. He ran up the stairs behind them. "Here I go! Take me one on one, pussies!" He was twirling around in circles, wanting someone to step up. "Come on!" He began walking up and down the tier. He heard a few snickers but other than that everyone was acting as if they didn't see him. The next thing he knew he was being thrown to the floor, facedown, his wrists being handcuffed behind his back.

"Charade's over!" the burly Hulk Hogan wannabe in an officer's uniform said.

"I ain't do nothing man! I'm the one bleeding! Look at my back!" *Crack.* He was hit over the head.

"Shut the fuck up!" two of the other officers yelled at him.

"This is bullshit," Peanut mumbled as they picked him up and brisked him away.

That was almost three days ago. Now here he was, listening to this old man tell him some more bullshit.

"Youngblood, you need to watch your back. No pun intended. They're teasing you right now and at the same time testing your manhood." He was twirling a toothpick around in his mouth. He had a huge birthmark on the left side of his face that resembled a burn. His head was shaved clean. His droopy eyes and sagging jowls put about fifteen years on his fifty.

"Tell me something I don't know OG"

"What the hell you think I'm tryna do! If you ain't gittin' outta here today you better strike first. 'Cause it's not gonna be a teaser the next time." He swaggered over to the bottom bunk and laid down. He was an ex-Blood himself.

Peanut was now sitting all the way up, his feet dangling off the bed.

"Youngblood, take this." He passed him a bundle of cloth. Peanut grabbed it and unwrapped it. Running his hand over what used to be the top of a mop handle, it was now a shank, a piece of protection, a piece of mind. Not much, but it was something.

"I 'preciate this OG." Peanut got down and secured his protection. "OG?"

"What Youngblood? I'm tryna take a nap. You want me to show you how to use it too?" he snapped.

"Naw OG, I can handle it. I need to know where them other two niggas that came in with me are."

"How in the hell should I know?" He pulled the sheet over his head, then mumbled, "They got discharged."

* * *

Peanut finally decided to tell it all to Shan. She picked up on the first ring. After the operator said "Go ahead, sir," Peanut caught a lump in his throat.

"Peanut . . . Peanut . . ." Shan cried his name. "Please don't tell me you're hurt. Are they raping you? What happened? Why are you in jail? Peanut, you know you are all I got; don't do this to me. It's been four days since I heard from you, you could have called sooner." She rattled off.

"Shan! Shan! I'm cool. I'm okay. I just need you to handle some things so I can get the fuck outta here as soon as possible. A'ight?" Instead of answering she just kept on crying. "Shan you gonna help me or not?"

"Of course I'ma help you. What kind of bullshit question is that? Tell me what happened Peanut."

"Niggas tried to jack me at the wrong place at the wrong time. The po-po was everywhere to make a long story short. Brianna was the only other person who knew what was going down."

"How do she know your business?"

"That's a whole 'nother story. Patch me through to Keke. She got that damn block on the phone. She hasn't called you looking for me?"

"No."

"That bitch probably in Atlantic City somewhere celebrating the fact that I haven't been home. And I need you to pull yourself together."

"All right. All right. Hold on." She dialed Keke's number and after the voice mail kicked in Shan left a message saying Peanut was locked up and to call her ASAP. "I'ma go over there," she assured Peanut.

"Where the fuck is this bitch when I need her?" Peanut hissed. His pride was hurt. "Call Nick too."

"Just tell me what you need me to do. Fuck her! We all we got Peanut."

"I need a real lawyer, like yesterday. I declined the fake ass pretender they tried to give me. Tell that bitch to give you that 20Gs she holding for me."

"Got you."

Peanut then gave her the rest of the info on his arrest and the numbers to a couple of people that was holding money for him.

His old lawyer that he had on retainer, they fell out and he just fired him. He gave Shan a number to another lawyer.

"You got all that?"

"I got it Peanut. Now can I get a word in?"

"What's up?"

"Are you okay?"

"I told you I'm straight."

"You didn't get into any fights?" She was talking like a concerned parent.

"I told you, I'm fine."

"That's not what I asked you!" she snapped.

"No fights. Listen. Stop worrying, a'ight. Just get me a lawyer so I can get the fuck outta here."

"One more question?" She heard him let out a huge sigh. "Look, boy. You all I got so I know I can be concerned. This will be my last question." She snapped.

"What is it?"

"Did they rape you?" Someone was trying to get through on her line.

Peanut let out a chuckle, which assured her that he was surviving. "You need to stop watching *Oz* and the rest of that shit. There are plenty of niggas willing to give up the ass. Niggas don't have to go around raping niggas."

Shan breathed a sigh of relief. "When are you gonna call me back?"

"Later. Love you."

"Love you too." Shan hung up and checked her voice mail.

* * *

Nyla was sitting on the porch when her cell phone rang. When the operator said "Collect call from Peanut, Wayne County Jail," her eyes got so big her sister Lisha thought they were gonna pop out of their sockets.

"Who is that?"

Nyla waved her off and she got up and began walking. She didn't want her sister to be privy to the fact that she was talking to another man. "Yes. I'll accept. Peanut, what's going on with you?"

"I got caught up in some shit. I should be out in a couple of days. You a'ight? You need anything?"

Nyla laughed. "I should be asking you those questions. Let me send you some money."

"Nah. I'm straight. Like I said, I'll be out in a few." He was relishing the sound of her voice and was imagining running his fingers through her locks.

"I want to. That way I won't keep feeling guilty for accepting money from you. If my husband ever found out . . . well, I can't even *fathom* the outcome." She let out a nervous laugh.

"The only way he'll find out is if you tell. Plus, I already told you to look at it as a gift."

"Yeah, right. A gift of money from the next nigga! If your wifey did that, how would you respond?" Peanut laughed. "That's what I thought. Plus I'm already being accused of wanting to move on to the next nigga."

"So ya'll two doing a'ight, or what?"

"Considering the circumstances, we're maintaining."

"Aww, dayumn. That wasn't the answer I was looking for." Nyla blushed. "Look, can I see you next weekend?"

"Peanut you know that wouldn't be a good idea. I got a husband, you got a wife. I enjoyed our conversations but you know the sayings: all good things must eventually come to an end and don't play with fire and expect not to get burnt."

"So you're going to end our friendship?"

"Umm-hmm. I know you can respect that."

Peanut allowed a few seconds of silence to elapse before saying, "A'ight. I'ma give you that."

"Thank you. Take care of yourself Peanut." Nyla remained standing in place in deep thought with her back to Lisha.

"Who is Peanut?" Lisha was standing behind her with her hands on her hips.

Shan checked her voice mail and was surprised to hear Briggen's voice. She immediately called him back.

"Hey." Her voice trembled.

"Hey to you too!"

"Glad to hear that you are alive. You scared me and I don't appreciate that."

Briggen chuckled then coughed. "Damn."

"Sorry about that."

"Naw. It's not you. It hurts when I cough, when I laugh, hell, even hurts to breathe. But shit, at least I'm living, and you're living, am I right?"

"Yeah, you're right. How many bullets did you take?"

"Three."

"Three?" Shan gasped.

"It's not as bad as it sounds. One went through me and you are lucky it didn't hit you. I wouldn't have been able to forgive myself."

"Oh my God!" Shan cried out. "Calvin, I—"

"Hey. It's over. It's all good." He cut her off. "No need to worry about it. Now when are you gonna come and check on a sick man?"

"Nigga don't even try it! All of them—"

"Look at you. A second ago you were in tears apologizing. In a matter of seconds you switched to bitch mode."

Shan smiled. "Like I said; don't even try it. You probably got two bitches there right now. What? They went to get you something to eat so that's how you were able to sneak a call in to me? I can't fuck with you Briggen."

"I don't have to sneak and do nothing. I'ma grown-ass man. Just say the word and I'll make sure ain't nobody here but me and you. You need to come and check on a sick man. It's almost time for my sponge bath."

That image alone caused Shan's pussy to wake up. But she immediately shook it off. "I told you. I can't fuck with you like that."

"Come on now. Make a sick man happy. I saved your life remember? That deserves me getting a visit from you; in a candy striper's outfit, no panties, and a sponge bath. That's a fair exchange."

That got a laugh outta Shan. "Nigga you don't give up do you?"

"Not when it's something I'm after."

"Let me think about it okay?"

"What's there to think about?"

"I told you. I got a big problem with all of them hoes you got."

"Girl I told you they run my businesses."

"Plus, I'm talking to somebody. Hold on. I'm expecting another call."

"From him?"

"No, from my brother's girl." She clicked over and it was Keke. "Girl, you saved me. Where have you been? Don't go nowhere; let me get rid of this nigga." She clicked back over. "Briggen that's her. I'm glad that you're okay, for real. I gotta run."

She hung up not allowing him to respond. Then she filled Keke in on what was going on with her brother.

16

SHADEE

After they formulated a plan, Sha and his crew spent the next two hours cleaning up the place and deciding the best way to handle the situation. Finally Shadee took Janay, Kay-Gee, the dope, the money and left. The rest of the crew were left behind to get rid of the bodies and torch the building. The three of them rode in silence all the way to Kay-Gee's where Shadee dropped him and the dope off.

As he headed for his house he kept glancing over at Janay who sat balled up into a knot. She didn't utter a sound as she stared out the window.

Janay could not believe what she had just been through in the last seventy-two hours. She banged her head up against the headrest and she replayed the events of the last three days. Her two bodyguards, who were also her cousins, Jeff K and Biz, was just sittin' around chillin' and servin' through the dope slot on the door. She noticed that Biz was a little edgy that evening. When the knock came that got shit started, Biz answered the door. When he came back he told them that there was some peeps wanting to get served some nice weight. Janay had said no. Jeff K was agreeing with her. Biz was persistent and finally blurted out that he would vouch for them and to go ahead and serve them. Janay finally gave in and when Biz opened the door there were three slimy-looking cats. Soon as they got inside they drew their weapons and the tall one warned, "Y'all know what time it is." Jeff K, wasting no time, fired first. Janay dove to the floor, crawled to the sofa and got her gun. She automatically went to shooting and didn't stop until her gun was the only one being heard. When it got quiet and she peeked over the sofa, Jeff K and one of the robbers were down. Biz was yelling because he was hit in the leg. She was so busy releasing fire power she didn't know when the other two robbers escaped. She then jumped up and locked the door.

"I'm hit Janay! I'm fuckin' hit Janay!" Biz screamed and tried to get up but Janay kicked him twice in the stomach.

"You fuckin' snake! You ain't no good Biz! How could you? We family, you skank motherfucker!" She kicked him again.

"What you talkin' about Janay? What's the matter with you?"

She went over to Jeff K and was trying to feel a pulse. "He's dead Biz. Damn it! Damn it!" She stomped.

"You act like my bullet is what did it!" he screamed out.

"Your punk ass, you could've stopped it! It might as well had been your bullet. You let those bastards in! What was your cut? You greedy bastard! How much was you gonna get?" She was now throwing things at him, she was so furious.

"No fire was supposed to go off!" Biz argued, while trying to duck the objects.

"What was your cut?"

"Jeff fired first Janay!"

"Of course he did! What did you think, he was gonna stand there and let us get robbed! You know what?" she screamed. "Naw, fuck it!" She gave him the hand. "I got somethin' for your bitch ass. Help me move these bodies!"

"Fuck them! Let's get the fuck outta here!"

"Boy, you betta get your punk ass up and help me move these bodies." She warned.

"I'm hit Janay, damn!"

"Big fuckin' deal! Jeff is dead." The tears were streaming down her cheeks.

With that said and Biz seeing that there was no way out of it, he forced himself up, limping, and he helped Janay move the tall robber who Biz said was named Winston. Then it was Jeff K's turn. As they carried his body to the back, Janay started gagging. She let go of his legs and let Biz drag him by himself.

"Place him facedown," she ordered.

"What difference does it make?"

"Place him facedown, Biz!" He did it but mumbled, "It don't make no damn difference."

As he turned him over Janay aimed her gun at him. "It does make a difference." When he turned around she put two holes in his chest. "This is for family, nigga."

Immediately afterwards she began calling Shadee. When she couldn't get him she called her sister Crystal who panicked. Which is the main reason Big Choppa never put her in charge. It took Janay almost an hour to calm her down. She didn't really sweat it because she needed to talk to someone. She finally decided on staying put until Shadee made it over because he would know what to do.

She turned and looked over at Shadee who was intensely staring at the road. "Are you sure they're gonna handle everything?" She was watching him with hopeful eyes and was practically holding her breath.

"Yeah. I'm sure."

Janay let out a huge sigh of relief. "Thanks babee." Then blurted out, "I got a new body on my hands."

"It's over Janay. Learn to let go."

When they pulled up in front of Shadee's crib, Doc was sitting on the porch looking pissed off. Janay was surprised that he wasn't around when everything went down.

"Where was Doc, your right hand man?"

Shadee sucked his teeth. "I don't know where that nigga been."

They stepped out of the car and headed up the walkway. Doc didn't get up; he just stared at Shadee.

"Hey Doc," Janay said.

"What's up?" He stood up.

Shadee didn't say anything as he unlocked the door and they all went inside.

"You a'ight?" Doc asked Janay.

"I guess so," she mumbled.

Janay really didn't want to be left home alone. Plus, she wasn't ready to go into detail and explain to Shadee all the shit she was into. Not yet. And with Doc there she knew Shadee was getting ready to hit the streets. So she went in the bedroom and grabbed a change of clothes. She was relieved that she hadn't drove her car over to the projects but instead rode with Jeff K.

"Shadee, I'm going over Mama's. Make sure you lock up."

"I just gotta make a quick run. I need you to stay put until I get back. We gotta talk. You gave me your word that you wasn't gonna hustle no more. You got some explainin' to do. I'll be right back."

"Sha, don't start. You know damn well a quick run could mean days. I don't want to be by myself. Come pick me up whenever you finish and we'll talk then." Without waiting for a response she slipped out the door.

"Janay!" Shadee yelled after her. "I'ma fuck that bitch up."

She ignored him, and jumped in her ride and sped off. She only got two blocks away from her house when she had to pull over. As soon as she shut the engine off, she burst out crying. She still could not believe the chain of events that took place over the last seventy-two hours. She kept mulling over the fact that she fo-real, foreal had a new body on her hands and her cousin was gone. Her mother's oldest brother's baby son, Jeff K, was dead. She wasn't up to bearing that bad news and was still undecided as to if she should even tell them. She was resting her head on the steering wheel and was now crying uncontrollably. She almost jumped outta her skin when an elderly woman tapped on the glass. "I'm fine!" Janay blurted out before the woman could ask her what the problem was. Janay didn't even look at her as she started the car, turned it around and headed back to her house.

Shadee's Benz and Doc's Range Rover were still in the driveway. Janay, finding a spot to park, hopped outta the car and hurried up the walkway. She turned the knob because she knew she hadn't locked it on her way out. She hoped that Shadee didn't have to go out after all, because she was now feeling a deep rooted need to unburden everything that had happened. She threw her purse onto the couch and headed straight for the bathroom. A tub full of hot water and chamomile oil was screaming for her smelly, tired, aching body. All she wanted was to soak, smoke a blunt with a glass of wine or two and for Shadee to hold and comfort her. The closer she got to the bathroom, the clearer she could hear sounds of someone getting fucked but she couldn't put her finger on it. "I know my fuckin' neighbor don't got her skank ass up in my house!" She knew that *only* Sha and his boy where supposed to be in her house. When she got to Sha's bedroom she placed her ear up against the door.

"Fuck me man," Doc begged. But Janay wasn't sure if that's what he said or not. His voice sounded different. The growls they were making sounded as if they were possessed.

Janay turned the doorknob and quietly cracked the door. "Oooh!" she gasped, her eyes going wide in shock. So surprised was she that her feet had somehow become glued to the floor. All she could do was stare in horrified fascination at the two big niggas buck ass naked. Shadee was leaned up against the dresser with his head back, eyes closed with both hands on Doc's head. Doc's head was bobbing up and down as he was on his knees sucking Shadee's dick as if he was a crack bitch and was promised a rock if she did a good job.

"Oh, my God!" Janay's mind screamed out as she watched them enjoy each other, not quite believing what was going on before her eyes.

"Fuck me Sha," Doc was saying in between slurps. "Fuck me now."

Shadee acted as if he had an attitude because he sucked his teeth and ordered, "Get up, bitch ass nigga."

Doc had this slick smirk on his face as he got up off his knees and got on the bed on his hands and knees. "Fuck me Daddy. Give me that big ass dick. You said it belonged to me."

Janay was getting sick as she saw her man get in position right behind Doc's ass and ram his dick so hard into his ass hole that she wanted to say ouch. But instead of Doc screaming out as if he was in pain, his eyes closed and he was groaning and throwing that ass back at Shadee, who had sweat dripping off his body, enjoying it just as much as Doc seemed to be.

Janay closed the door back and made a dash for the bathroom, barely making it before she began to vomit. The nasty taste of bile was in her throat and mouth as she frantically began brushing her teeth. Then she abruptly stopped cold, realizing that Shadee was fucking Doc without a condom. She threw the toothbrush down and ran to her room with intentions on getting her gun. But when she got there and closed the door, her mind went blank. *What the fuck? What the fuck am I supposed to do now?* Her heart was pounding so hard she thought her chest was going to burst. "I'ma fuckin' kill this nigga!" She went into her closet and pulled out a Smith & Wesson that her pops had given her. When she went to open her door, Sha was stepping out of the bedroom talking on his celly as if he just got done taking a shit. He had his boxers on.

"Nigga how you gonna disrespect me like that?" Doc was coming behind him pulling up his pants. He was carrying his shirt, following behind Shadee who was motioning to Doc to shut up because he was interrupting his phone conversation; but Doc kept going off about being disrespected. When Sha finally flipped the cell phone closed. He started going off.

"Man, why the fuck you soundin' like a bitch? We fuckin' partnas, we ain't man and wife!" Shadee pushed Doc backwards. "You got me fucked up!"

"Oh shit!" Janay mumbled. She threw the gun on the bed, now unsure of what to do.

"Nigga how could you do this to me?" Doc was trying to rush Shadee and was yelling at him.

"Get the fuck outta my house dawg!" Shadee was trying to push him towards the door.

"I'm not going no-fuckin'-where! Shadee how could you do this to me?" He yelled, "Y'all have been seeing each other for how long? When did it start?" He was swinging at Shadee as if he was a bitch scorned.

"Get the fuck out man! I'm not going to tell you again," Shadee warned.

"Nigga, I've been nothin' but true to you. Fuckin' bitches, I could deal with it. We had that understanding Sha. But Bishop? You fucked him and Demetrick. That fake ass nigga?"

Popow! Shadee punched him twice in the face. His nose gushed out blood. "You wanna be a bitch?" Shadee kept pimp slapping him. "I told you we ain't man and wife."

"Shadee!" Janay yelled as she ran out of her bedroom. Shadee's eyes got so big she thought they were gonna pop outta the sockets. But Doc didn't give a shit. He just kept on bitchin'.

Sha was pushing Doc down the stairs and to the door. "Fuck you Sha!" Doc yelled as the door slammed in his face. He immediately began bangin' on the door. "Girlfriend, if you want to live a long time, do not give him no pussy!" He screamed like a bitch, then started laughing. "That dick has been up in a little bit of everybody! You gonna get yours nigga!" *Plop! Plop!* Two bullets soared through the door, one barely missing Shadee's arm, the other one lodged into Janay's family photo.

"What the fuck was that Sha?" She wasted no time digging in Shadee's shit, not caring about the bullets. Her head was spinning and her voice was cracking.

"You heard it all." He stormed towards her and grabbed her by the neck. "Now we both got a secret: you got a fresh body on your hands and I fuck niggas in the ass! And this better not go no further than this room. You understand?" Janay was gasping for air and tears were running down her cheeks. "Do you understand me?" She shook her head yes hoping he would let her go. "Good." As soon as he let her go she went to swinging.

"You motherfuckin' bitch ass hoe!" She screamed as she slapped him in the face. "You fuck every bitch that walks but that isn't enough. You had to go fuck niggas, too?" She was close enough to get a grip so she dug her fingernails into his face. He slammed his fist up against the bottom of her chin. She let him go and was crying so loud his ears was ringing. She fell to her knees and was looking up at him. "I saw you fuck him, and I heard him Shadee. Loud and clear. I didn't want to hear him but I did. You fuckin' more than one nigga! I heard him. You infected ain't you?" She howled. "How could you do this to me? You hate me that much?" she cried. "Oh, God, why, Shadee?"

When he picked her up off the floor she was kicking and screaming. It looked as if her eyes were rolling up into her head. He tried to lay her down on the couch but she was going wild. He finally slapped her in the face.

"Janay!" he yelled. "Janay!" He slapped her again.

She stopped kicking and was trying to get a grasp on her crying. "Why, Shadee? Babee, why? We have a son together."

"Get tested, Janay. You probably don't even have it. The few times in the past few months that we fucked we used protection." He attempted to soothe her.

"Not every time!" she screamed. "Damn, Sha! You are my son's father," she cried in disbelief.

"Get tested Janay. I doubt if you have it."

"Shadee. What is the matter with y'all? You have to conquer the world? Huh? Is that it? What is up with y'all fine ass, thuggish niggas fuckin' each other? I thought Doc was your right hand man? Shit! He looks like Suge Knight. I thought y'all was gangsta! What is the matter with y'all? Huh? Explain this shit to me! Doc has a woman and kids!" She had jumped up and was standing in his face. "Y'all get all the pussy in the world thrown at y'all. Wassup G?" She was walking hard like a dude.

"Girl, go 'head." He was walking away.

"Go 'head? That's all you got to say?" She followed behind him as he grabbed his keys and stormed out the door.

17

SHAN AND PEANUT

"Keke, why in the fuck did you tell me to come over at nine knowin' damn well you wasn't gonna be home?" Shan yelled into the phone. Her frustration level was at an all time high. Keke was Peanut's wifey and she was pressed to pick up the twenty grand she was holding for him.

"My bad Shan. I'll be there by eleven so come . . ."

"Whatever. I'm home in the bed." *Click.* Shan slammed the phone down, cutting her off. She couldn't wait to tell Peanut that Keke, along with everybody else on his team, had been giving her the run-around about his money. That's how niggas do when you get knocked. And that's what she had expected, so she now had to do what she had to do.

As soon as she got comfortable and reached over and turned off her nightlight the phone rang. She started not to answer but thinking and hoping that maybe it would be her brother she grabbed the receiver. She really needed to hear his voice. "Hello."

"Shan, please don't hang up this time! I know I fucked up and if I could take it all back I—"

"Brianna, now is not the time. But I will be by your house in the morning on my way to work." *Click.* With that said, that's the second bitch who got hung up on in the last hour. Brianna had been calling her nonstop wanting to apologize and explain to Shan why she did what she did. Even though Shan missed her best friend, the shit she'd done was totally unacceptable and unforgivable. *How could I have been so blind? How could I have been so stupid? B, from day one, was a snake and I couldn't even see it! How could she do me like this? We grew up together, the sister I never had. Some sister!* Shan couldn't stop thinking about how low the people closest to you would go as she cried herself to sleep.

That next morning before heading over to Brianna's she decided to pay Keke a surprise visit. At a quarter past eight she was knocking on her front door. Peanut and Keke had had this three bedroom home on the East Memphis for almost two and a half years. Shan knocked harder and rang the bell again. Keke was a baller, the only type of hoes that Peanut would fuck with. All his women at one time or another were in the game. Just as Shan turned to go back to her car the door opened.

"Whassup?" she heard from a deep voice.

Surprised that another nigga would be answering the door, Shan stared at him for a minute. One, because she was starstruck. Two, because Keke got a lot of nerve to have another nigga all up in her brother's house. "Um . . . Is Keke home? Tell her Shan is here." The rapper Project Pat was probably wondering why she was standing there with her mouth open.

"Keke!" he yelled. "You got company!" Then, turning to Shan, "You comin' in or what?" He held the door open for Shan. "Have a seat."

"Thanks," Shan muttered, still confused as to why this rap nigga was all up in her brother's crib acting like he was legal. On top of that she thought that he was locked up. When he disappeared up the stairs, Keke came down. She looked as if she had just woke up, coupled with the fact of Shan showing up, her eyes were big with surprise.

"Shan, what's up girl?"

"You tell me what's up! My brotha ain't been locked up a

month and you got niggas all up in his spot. That's totally disrespectful." Shan had to slip that in. "You got my brother's money?"

"Girl, he just came b—"

"And I just came by to pick up my brother's money. You ain't got to explain shit to me." Shan cut her off.

"Oh. Well, your brother and—"

"I told you, Keke, I ain't tryna hear that so save the explanations for your man. I got another stop to make so just give me my brother's money!"

Keke rolled her eyes, turned and sauntered up the stairs. Pat came down the stairs and went in the kitchen. Keke came down shortly afterwards and handed her a manila envelope.

Noticing how small it was, Shan asked, "How much is this?"

"Twenty-five hundred."

"Twenty-five hundred?! Peanut said you had twenty grand! Where is the rest?"

"That's all I was holding for *him*."

Shan couldn't help but laugh. "Bitches ain't shit! But you know what? I'ma let him deal with you. I'm out!"

"Hold up Shan. Pat you got some money on you?" She yelled into the kitchen.

"What you say?"

"How much money you got on you?" He came out of the kitchen, digging in his pockets. He pulled out some bills, shelled out a thousand dollars, gave it to her and went back into the kitchen.

"Here. That's thirty five hundred."

"Bitch, please! Is this supposed to make me jump up and down with joy? This is a far cry from twenty grand." Shan stormed out, leaving no doubt that she was pissed and headed for Brianna's.

"Can things get any more fucked up than they already are? Why me?" Shan muttered to herself, maneuvering through the morning traffic. She needed ten thousand for Peanut's bond, twenty-five thousand for the lawyer's fee and he's charging her another five to get him transferred to another county jail. At the thought of all of that Shan was ready to snap as she pulled behind Brianna's Lex. "This bitch better be home!" Shan stuffed the envelope that Keke just gave her into the glove compartment and locked it. It had been a little over a week since she last saw Brianna and was tired of hanging up on her and listening to her whine and grovel. Before she could even knock on the door, it flew open. Brianna was standing there with a black scarf on her head, a faded black t-shirt and white boxers.

"Shan please, forgive me. I am *so* sorry. There is no excuse for what I've done and I take full responsibility." She wasted no time getting into her apology.

Pop! Shan hauled off and punched Brianna in the mouth, causing her to fall back onto the couch. Shan closed the front door and locked it. Even though she had on a skirt, she kicked off her shoes, sat her bag down and jumped on Brianna. A shocked Brianna could do nothing but block the blows and cover her face and head the best she could. "Bitch . . . fight me back . . . so that I can have an excuse . . . to kill your scandalous ass . . . !" Those words hurt more than the ass whipping itself. Shan kept beating her until she was out of breath, then fell back against the love seat. The same love seat her and Brianna would kick back, eat ice cream, gossip and watch movies on.

Brianna was balled up into a knot on the floor crying quietly and sniveling like a child. "Sshhhan . . . I'm sorry."

"Bitch please! Sorry is not gonna undo what you've done to my brother. My *brother* Brianna!" She grabbed the ashtray and hurled it at her, hitting her shoulder. Brianna wailed like a wounded animal. "My brother has always been good to you. We treated you like family. Why Brianna? I never judged you. I never knocked your hustle, so why? I know you wasn't that hard up for money! You could have asked me for whatever!" Shan's voice was trembling and all she could see was fire. "Tell me why you had to do that to him." Shan sat glaring at Brianna and waiting for a response. All she got was more sniveling. She looked around the apartment and it looked as if Brianna hadn't left out or cleaned up in days.

Pizza boxes, Chinese food containers, chips were all over the table and floor. "This place is disgusting and so are you! Peanut's bail is twenty-five thousand. Give it up!"

That request caused Brianna to raise her head up. "I don't have that kind of money," she barely got out.

"Hoe, I know you got something, so don't even try to play me. I ain't the one Brianna. If you really meant what you said about being sorry you would have been trying to get that shit up. What do you have now? The lawyer ain't gonna do shit without something." Brianna just lay there on the floor sobbing. "Get your ass up! Go get me something! I gotta stop by the lawyer's office before I go to work."

Brianna slowly got up off the floor. "I'm sorry Shan. If I could take it all back, I—"

"Brianna," Shan interrupted, "save the theatrics and just go get the cash." When Brianna finally came back she handed Shan some bills. Shan, again feeling how light they were asked, "What the fuck is this?"

Brianna shamefully said, "Fourteen hundred. I told you I ain't have no money. This is everything I got here."

Shan just shook her head in disgust. "All this fuckin' you been doin'. All this settin' up the dope boys and you only got fourteen hundred to show for it? Brianna you either one, think I'm dumb or two, you dumber than fuck! You need to check yourself because you'll never, ever find a friend like me. You better get some more money up because I'll be back. So lay on that grimey ass back some more because you're *gonna* come up with some money. You're the one responsible for this whole fuckin' mess!" Then she hauled off and punched her in the face again. "And I know you fucked Kris!" Shan turned and left while ignoring Brianna's pleas to be forgiven.

Shan was deep in thought on her way to work. She stopped by the lawyer's office and gave him the thirty five hundred from Keke and Brianna's fourteen hundred. A very far cry from thirty thousand. The shiesty ass lawyer kept twenty five hundred for his retainer and the remaining twenty four hundred went towards getting Peanut transferred to another jail. "Fuck!" she said out loud. "Forever is going to have to come with it. And I mean soon."

When she arrived at work, being that this was an afternoon that she taught class, inmates were standing around her office. Some were waiting to ask questions, some wanting to know how soon they could get in her class and some were just waiting for her to unlock the computer room door. She had intentions on canceling class but since everyone around her was ready to get down to business she got herself together and tried to act as if she didn't have such heavy burdens on her shoulders.

Two and a half hours later, class was over, the halls were empty and Shan was able to make herself a cup of peppermint tea and wind down a little. She was checking her E-mail and sipping her tea when Forever tapped on the door.

"Come in."

"Why you say it like that? This *is* your open house. The door is supposed to be open. You sound like you mad cause you gotta be here," Forever told her.

"I know I can take a break!"

"How you gonna break during your open house hours?" he challenged.

"Don't tell me what to do. As a matter of fact, you can leave and come back in an hour. We need to talk."

"I'm here now. Talk." He grabbed the chair that was in front of her desk.

She started to object but then thought better of it. "I need money now."

"I told you I got you."

"When Forever? I need it now."

He could hear the desperation in her voice. *Damn, I really got this bitch's back up against the wall.* "How much you need?"

"Ten grand for my brother's bail, twenty-six hundred for the transfer and I still need the whole twenty-five thousand for the lawyer's fee."

"Goddamn girl." Then he said to himself, *I knew I had her, but damn!* Then his thoughts went to getting some pussy but he tossed them out. *I'ma get rich off of this bitch.*

Shan watched Forever as he was in deep thought. *Damn. Why couldn't this nigga be on the streets?* She slyly licked her lips as she anticipated him kissing her. He was the bomb kisser. He was giving out kisses that left her nipples hard, pussy wet and head dizzy. "So, what's up?" she inquired, breaking his thought pattern. She got up to reheat her tea. Her office was equipped with a microwave, small refrigerator and a coffeemaker.

"When you pick up the first package, I'll make sure the twenty-six hundred is with it."

Shan put the cup down, put a hand on her hip, a pout on her face and asked, "Why can't I have it all now? I'm good for it Forever. I'm in a bind."

"We gotta make it first. I can't give what I ain't got."

"Forever, don't even try it. I know you got it. I need it now."

He watched her ass as she bounced back to her chair. She started to sit down but changed her mind and came back around to the front of her desk. She leaned back against it ready to argue and convince him to give her the money now.

Before she could start, Forever said, "I'm serious Ma, we gotta make it first. I can give you the twenty-six hundred now. That's the best I can do." *That's all I'm gonna do for now. Fuck bitch ass Peanut.* She sucked her teeth and was looking at him to see if he was lying. Finally a tear fell. "Awwwww, dayuum girl. Don't start that crying shit." He bounced up, snatched a tissue out of the box and dabbed her cheek.

"I told you I needed this yesterday." She was staring in his eyes, not giving up. He was beginning to like that about her. "I need it now Forever."

"Look Ma. Listen to me. You said the twenty-six hundred will get him transferred. So at least he'll be a'ight for a minute. Next week I'll make sure you get the ten and he'll be out. You know he can hang in there for at least another week. Right?"

Shan thought about what he had said. "Next week?" She was hoping.

"I got you." He leaned in and kissed her lips lightly. "A'ight?" He leaned in and kissed her again.

This time she kissed him back. Hungrily. "You got me?" she whispered seductively.

"I said I got you." He pulled her skirt up and sat her on top of the desk. *Damn.* Forever was now talking to himself. *What's a nigga to do? Don't fuck her man. Don't do it.* That little voice was telling him. *You got her back up against the wall. She already on your team. She already down for whatever; you ain't got to fuck her man. I'm telling you. Walk away from this pussy. It's a bad business move with consequences that's gonna fuck you up! I'm telling you.* •

Shan kissed him some more and grabbed his dick. Sensing his hesitancy she began massaging it, causing it to stretch out. "What? You having second thoughts all of a sudden?" She teased and moaned as he grabbed her nipples. Shan had been dying to get the dick. The last time she got fucked was with Briggen. And that was a few months ago.

"What's a nigga to do?" he asked her. He was trying to be strong even though she was stretching him all the way out.

"I don't know. You tell me. I do know we don't have much time." She grabbed his hand, ran it up her thigh and landed it on her wet pussy. "You can have it if you want it. I know I want this." She squeezed him harder.

"Damn," he mumbled and moaned as she unzipped his pants and started maneuvering her panties off. There was no turning back now. Before you could count to three Forever was slidin' up in that pussy.

"Ohhh, aaaashit," was all Shan could squeak out. Forever spread her legs wider and placed one leg in the crook of his arm and tried to knock the bottom out.

Tap. Tap. Tap. "Ms. McKee." Someone was at her door.

A ball felt like it was caught in her throat and her eyes got big as saucers.

18

BRIANNA

After nursing the wounds from the ass whipping that Shan gave her, Brianna was determined to get her shit together. She had resolved to get her life together and do the right thing for once. Low as she had sunk she could go nowhere but up. Shan had been her family for years. Peanut had always treated her like a little sister—that is, until her hormones kicked in. She had always had a secret crush on Peanut. She would secretly eye him when he would be on the basketball court. She would be checking him out when he'd be on the corner slangin' rocks. She would especially love it when her and Shan would get into trouble and Peanut would come to their rescue. When she would spend the night over Shan's house she would get jealous when his girl-friends would sneak over and be in his room. Her and Shan would peep through the keyhole. Her fantasies would be of him caressing her all over her body and making her moan and quiver like the women in the movies.

They were only sixteen years old when Peanut moved out of their aunt's and got his own two bedroom apartment. Some weekends when Peanut had to go out of town, her and Shan would go over and spend the night. It made them feel grown and independent. He would leave money for them to go grocery shopping and pay them to clean up and do his laundry. They used to pretend that the apartment was their own and had planned on getting an apartment together as soon as they graduated from high school.

This one weekend while they were house sitting, around 2:30 in the morning Peanut stepped through the door. Brianna was chillin' in her favorite recliner watching TV.

"Why you back so soon?" Brianna, in actuality, was glad to see him. He stood six feet two, had light brown eyes with a huge afro. He was so fine to her and she always joked with Shan about how much they both looked like they were related to the Jackson family, back when Michael looked cute and black. "Y'all sure y'all not Joe Jackson's illegitimate children?" she would tease.

"What? Just because I let y'all spend the weekend I'm supposed to stay gone? I think y'all forgot whose spot this is."

"You can come home anytime you want. I was just asking," Brianna teased as she eyed Peanut as if he was a big, fat, juicy well done steak.

"'Where's big head?" he asked about Shan as he dropped his bag down and headed for the kitchen.

"She was out for the count by 1:00. You know that girl can't hang with me." Brianna got up and headed for the kitchen, too. Not bothering to cover up the nighty she was wearing, she was happy that Shan was asleep. The nighty was see-through, her 36C's were perked up and her ass cheeks were practically hanging out the bottom.

She sat at the table as she watched him throw together a turkey and cheese sandwich and grab a Heineken. He stopped and warned, "Don't be looking at my shit! Make your own."

"Who said I was hungry?" She sauntered over to the refrigerator, bending over, and came out with a Heineken. She peeked back and saw Peanut looking at her ass.

"Put that back! You ain't legal yet."

Brianna giggled. "I was just testing you."

"Yeah, right."

"Then let me have a sip of yours."

"Drink some Kool-Aid. And I know how many I got left so don't be slick." Peanut got up, grabbed his sandwich and beer and went to his room.

Brianna's hot ass was wetter than the ocean. She went and flopped back down into her favorite chair. She wasn't even watching the TV, the TV was watching her. She couldn't stop thinking about Peanut. Minutes and three fantasies later she heard music. She got up and tapped on Peanut's door. It was already cracked so she just pushed it open.

When he looked up and saw her he said, "Damn girl, why aren't you in bed?"

She didn't say anything. She went over to the rocking chair, moved the clothes out of it and sat down. She sat silently as she watched him in his boxers, roll a bag of weed. He had some reggae playing that she didn't recognize. When he finished he sat on the side of the bed and lit up a joint. She leaned back and threw one of her legs over the arm of the chair.

Peanut looked at the "I want to get fucked" expression on her face and then at her pussy poking out of the see-through panties and asked, "Whassup?"

"What you think nigga?"

Peanut grinned, knowing what time it was. "Girl, you know you jail bait. So don't even go there."

"Since when did that ever stop you?"

"What?"

"You heard me. You fucked Meshawn."

"She's legal."

"No she's not. She just told you that." Brianna opened her leg a little wider. "And I bet you she ain't better than me."

Fuck! Peanut said to himself. "You my sister's little girlfriend."

Brianna stood up and slowly pulled her nighty over her head. "Can't you see I'm not little anymore? Plus, I ain't like Meshawn; I know how to keep my mouth shut. That is, unless you *scared*."

Peanut laughed as he checked out this fully developed, tight assed body that was standing before him trying to seduce him.

"Put your gown back on girl. What you tryna do, get a nigga locked up?"

She picked up the nighty and seductively walked over to him and held it out to him. "You put it on me—that is, unless you *scared*," she challenged again.

"Girl, what is up with you? Tempting and enticing a nigga and shit! Keep fuckin' around and you just may get what you want." He didn't take the nightgown from her but found himself staring at the fine young work of art before him in living color.

She threw the nightgown over on the rocking chair and sat down on the bed. "Give me what I want Peanut."

"Girl, get outta here." When he grabbed her hand to pull her off the bed, she grabbed his dick and slid it out of his boxers. "I'm warning you, you can't handle this little girl."

She held it tight as she slowly sunk to her knees and wrapped her moist, succulent lips around the head. "Damn, girl, you ain't gonna give up are you?" He let her hand go while looking down at her. She now had his full attention as her tongue licked the tip and her lips sucked the head. "Who taught you how to do this?" Peanut grabbed her head with both hands, while guiding his dick in a little further. "Aaahh, yeah," Peanut hissed as Brianna's slurps were getting louder and louder. "Right there baby; just like that, keep . . . it . . . going." Brianna was having a field day, savoring the dick and the moment that she had been anticipating for years. "Hhh . . . hold up." He grabbed her head, slowly pullin' his dick out. "Shit girl, I was about to bust! Who the fuck you been practicing on?"

Brianna smiled at him, while licking her lips. "You got some good dick." She reached up and, grabbing his hand, she placed it on her wet pussy. "You see what you did to me?" The crotch of her panties was soaked as he rubbed two fingers up and down from her clit to the bottom of her pussy. He listened to deep moans escape as she leaned back and raised her legs. "Daddy, please do something with this," she begged.

"What you want me to do?" he asked as he inserted two fingers inside her.

"Ooooohhhh," she groaned.

"What you want me to do?" he asked her again, making that pussy wetter and wetter.

"Fuck me, please. Fuck me! Shit, Peanut, fuck mmmmee." She was now on the verge of cuming.

He pulled off his boxers with his other hand, not stopping the action with her pussy. "You still want this?"

"Yes, Daddy, give it to me now," she moaned.

He pulled his fingers out just as her pussy was beginning to contract. "Noooooo." She arched her back and opened her eyes. "Don't stop. Don't do me like this." She panicked thinking he was gonna change his mind but relaxed when Peanut rolled her panties down over her thighs.

He spread her legs wide and threw a leg over his shoulder. The next thing she felt was the head of his dick teasing her clit. That shit was having her climb the walls. "You like that don't you?" He was looking at her shaking her head wildly. "You gonna like this even better." When he put just the head in a whole lot of hot pussy juice oozed out. They both let out moans at the same time. Peanut's dick went crazy as her pussy yanked him all the way up inside.

"Oh, Peanut, baby, this feels sooo good," she mumbled as she matched her rhythm to his.

"This is what you wanted right?" He slapped her ass.

"Ooh, yesssss . . . Daddy."

Peanut dug into her young pussy as if he would never fuck again. It was squeezing his dick, smothering it in hot wet pussy juice as she started cuming. He couldn't control himself no longer as he stroked one more time, plunging into ecstasy, releasing what felt like everything he had, then collapsing on top of her.

Brianna lay there smiling as her fantasy had finally come true. Ever since that day, eight years ago, whenever she wanted it, she could always get it. Whenever he wanted it he could always get it. That was one secret she never told Shan.

* * *

Brianna was sitting at the kitchen table drunk, and kicking herself in the ass for tearing down the only real two relationships she had built and enjoyed for the last thirteen years. Those loving relationships she had with Shan and Peanut came tumbling down in a matter of forty-eight hours. *I gotta do something.*

Her thoughts flashed back to the night her and Shan went to the club. She discreetly left the club with Peanut, giving Shan the impression that she was leaving with Skye. Three nights later Peanut showed up about 1:30 in the morning talking about how hungry he was. Brianna was glad to see him and pulled out the leftover baked ziti and garlic bread. Then she threw together some salad and poured him a glass of wine and let him go for what he knew.

After he finished eating, she washed the few dishes and put them away before joining him in the living room.

"I need you to do something for me." He said while patting the spot next to him.

Brianna instead sat on his lap. "What does Daddy need me to do?" she purred as she planted kisses on his face.

"I need you to make a run for me on Friday."

"You what!" She snapped her neck back, wanting to make sure she heard him right.

"I need you to make a run for me."

"Does this have something to do with that phone call you got when you was in the shower the other night?"

"Why? You was ear hustling?"

"I didn't have to ear hustle Peanut. The nigga was practically screaming!"

"You gonna do this for me or what?"

"Nigga please. For real? I'm insulted that you even asked me that!" She got up off his lap and headed for the kitchen.

"Why you can't do this one thing for me? I gotta go outta town."

She stopped dead in her tracks, turned around and yelled.

"Nigga, get one of them little lowlife hood rats that you be fuckin' with! What do I look like? You really got me fucked up Peanut. You just showed me what you really think about me, to ask me to do some shit like that."

"All the shit I do for you and the one time I ask you to do something for me, you gotta trip. Shit, I should be the one insulted."

"Fuck you! Get your wifey to make the motherfuckin' run if you so goddamn insulted!" she screamed.

"Ya know what?" Peanut stood up. " You is an ungrateful bitch. You know that right? It'll be a cold motherfuckin' day in hell before I ever do something for your hoe ass again. I'm out!"

"Fuck you, Peanut, and the dopin' ass, ugly bitch you got. She the hoe and you don't even see it. Ask her to make the run and watch what she tell your trick—" before she could get another word in, his fist was in her mouth and she was gagging on her bitten tongue.

"Bitch, you better watch your fuckin' mouth! You got me fucked up!" Peanut stormed out, almost tearing the door off its hinges when he left.

"You black bastard!" Brianna spat a mouth full of blood into her hand. She ran to the bathroom and looked in the mirror and screamed when she saw her gorgeous money-making Ms. America smile disappear under two grossly swollen lips. She ran to the front window to catch him, but all she saw was the taillights of his car. "I hate you!" she yelled out, yanking down the blinds. "I swear I'ma get his ass back!" She paced back and forth holding her mouth as if her teeth were going to fall out. "Fuck him and that dope sellin' bitch of his!" she cursed. Then it hit her. She went back into the bathroom to get a washcloth and filled it with some ice to place on her swollen lips. The tears were streaming down her cheeks as she periodically glared at a loose tooth. "This face and smile is my money-maker, muthafucker!" she said into the mirror. "I got something for your ass!" Her conscience was saying *don't do it Brianna.*

Fuck him! She paced back and forth. *I don't need his ass. I know one thing; I'ma get mines regardless.* She went hunting for her cell phone. When she found it, she punched in the numbers. The more it rang the madder she got.

"Yeah."

"Skye?" She wasn't sure if it was him.

"Yeah. Who dis?"

"It's me, Brianna," she said as if he should already know. "Nigga, I know you ain't forget me. I'm hanging the fuck up, I'm so insulted."

"Hold up. Hold up. I had to catch your voice. I know who this is. I called your fine ass a couple of times. What's up?"

"Money. You ready to make some?"

"I'm always ready. What you got?"

"Come see me."

"A'ight. Give me an hour."

She had been paging Nick and leaving him voice mail messages but he was not getting back to her. Shadee had not been by or returned her calls and Shan still wasn't speaking to her. Her own mother and sister had cut her off years ago. *So what if she slept with her sister's husband? Wasn't blood supposed to be thicker than water?* So, tomorrow Brianna would start packing. Her life, as she now knew it, would be just a memory. She saw no other way out.

She picked up the envelope off the table that was addressed to Shan. It wasn't sealed because she was unsure if she should send it to her. Was it too mushy? Too short? It seemed as if something was missing. She scanned through it once, then decided to read it out loud.

"Dear Shan,

I thank you for all of the pleasant memories we shared throughout the years. I thank you for the sisterly love and affection you smothered me with from day one. You are and will always remain my true sister.

For what it's worth, I am sorry for sleeping with Kris, even sorrier for what I did to Peanut. Since you will never see or hear from me again, I guess that now is the best time to tell you that I've always had a crush on him since the fourth grade. Well, by the eleventh grade, I finally was able to fulfill my fantasy. It happened during one of the weekends we house sat the apartment. We had been sneaking around ever since. Shan, please don't be mad at him and don't tell him I told you. I initiated the whole charade, so please, please don't be mad at him. Shit, from that day on, I made sure he could get it whenever or however he wanted it. That bitch Keke ain't shit! I don't know what he sees in that dope sellin' bitch. I tried to tell him that and we ended up exchanging words and he said some really foul shit to me. I was past mad. So, being the scandalous bitch that I am, I told his business to a jack boy. I swear Shan, if I would have known that shit was going to go down like it did, I would have acted out my anger and hurt differently. I pray that God forgives me, as well as Peanut and you.

I am thankful for you coming into my life. You taught me and showed me the meaning of true friendship. You never judged me, you never knocked my hustle. And for that, you'll never know how much that meant to me.

Everyone comes into our lives for a reason, season, or a lifetime. You will, for a lifetime, always be in my heart. I will miss you dearly.

My sugar daddy, Nick . . . Yeah, I know. I can see you with your hand on your hip saying, "No, this bitch ain't fuckin' with Nick again." Yes, I am. He's the only one who will put up with my bullshit. Anyways, he has some property in Florida. I'm going with him to start over with a clean slate. I gotta get right with God in order to get right with myself. Yes. You heard right. I said get right with God. But before I had the chance to get right with God, I had to hit one more lick. You know that nigga Link? He got that white hoe named Sunday. Well, that bitch is scandalous. She asked me if I was down to get paid; I told her of course. All I had to do was let him get me into the crib, unlock the back door and she had given me the code to deactivate the alarm. So you know that was a piece of cake for me. I don't know how much the hoe took but she gave me 7Gs. I'm enclosing a cashier's check for you to use for Peanut. By the time you get this letter I should be or I hope to be gone. I'm just waiting on the call from Nick.

In my heart for a lifetime,
Love, B"

"Damn." Brianna mumbled. Then laughed, "What the fuck am I crying for?" She wiped her tears with the back of her hand. Just as she folded the letter up and stuffed it and the check inside the envelope the phone rang.

"Nick, this better be yo' ass!" Brianna snapped as she ran for the phone.

"This is the Vartec operator. I have a collect call from Peanut. Will you accept?"

Brianna dropped the phone and stood there looking at it as if it was a snake. "Shit!" All types of thoughts were running through her head. But the emotion of guilt overshadowed everything. She picked up the phone and hung it up. She stood there knowing it was going to ring again. Sure enough, a few minutes later the operator was back on the line. This time Brianna accepted. God was telling her that she needed to ask for Peanut's forgiveness.

"Peanut?" She burst our crying.

"Bitch! It's too late to be sheddin' tears." His voice sounded deadly and she could feel the cold vibes through the phone as her arms got chill bumps. Then he broke out in a maniacal laughter. "You set up the wrong nigga!" He laughed some more. "You can forget about that call you're expectin' from Nick. That nigga is history! Even though ya'll both slimy and deserve each other. But he's history." Peanut was pissed at Nick because he had left him high and dry.

Brianna's breathing became sporadic as she tried to digest what he had just said. He had went back to that maniacal laughter. "W-what are you talkin' about, Peanut?"

"Bitch! I didn't stutter. You heard exactly what I said and you heard me right. I'll see you when I see you!"

Bbbzzzzzzzzzz. All she heard was dial tone.

19

SHAN

"Oh, shit!" Shan pushed Forever back. "Just a minute!" She hollered to whomever was at the door. Forever put his dick in his pants, reached down and snatched up her underwear. She grabbed them from him and went behind her desk and sat down.

"Come in."

The tall white inmate slowly eased the door open and peeked in before he stepped inside her office. He looked just as embarrassed as Shan. Forever was sitting in the chair, calm, as if nothing had happened.

"Uh, um, Ms. McKee, I'm just dropping off this convalescent slip for my roommate Torres. He had knee surgery."

Shan held out her hand to take the slip. "Thank you."

As the tall white guy turned to leave Forever said, "You stay in the unit with my boy Swap, right?"

"Yeah dude, why?"

"What's your name?"

"They call me Teko."

"I'm Forever." He got up and gave him dap. "Tell Swap I'ma holla at him later on."

"All right, cool." Teko left out.

That was Forever's way of issuing a silent threat. If any rumors began to circulate, Forever was going to start with Teko's ass. What Teko may have thought he walked in on and interrupted, needed to stay with Teko.

"Shit Forever!" Shan's heart was beating a mile a minute as she got up to put her panties back on.

"Hold up! Come on girl! What you doing?" He got up and locked the door.

"What does it look like? You tryna get me fired? Have you forgot where we are?"

He reached up and snatched the panties. "Naw, I ain't forget, but I know you gonna let me finish what we was into!"

"Forever, have you forgot where we are?"

Forever didn't respond verbally but physically he turned her towards the desk and bent her over. He pulled up her skirt, admiring and massaging her voluptuous ass before spreading her legs. Shan was now ready to get fucked again, and peeked over her shoulder in an attempt to see what Forever was doing. "Nigga, we gonna do this, or what?" Then she let out a loud gasp as Forever plunged all the way inside her.

"Yeah . . . we . . . gonna . . . do . . . this," he panted while gearing up to last as long as he could.

The only sounds that were heard was the two of them moaning. They both were trying to savor the moment. Shan, because she hadn't been fucked in months and on top of that she was actually diggin' him. Forever, because he hadn't been able to get some pussy, uninterrupted, in a long time and Shan was the shit.

"Go hhharder," Shan ordered, as she threw it at him a little faster. "Oh, shit, Forever! Just like . . . that!" She screamed as she grabbed onto the desk tighter, her stomach fluttered as her pussy began contracting while she burst a nice long nut. Her juices continued to seep out as Forever kept smashin' the pussy the way he wanted to. Shan forgot where she was. So did Forever when he raised one of her legs and rested her knee on the desk. "Oh, my Gggggod! I'm cummmin' again!" This time Forever came with her.

After he caught his breath, he placed kisses on the back of her neck. "Damn, you was good." He pulled out, then helped her up off the desk. They both fixed their clothes. "You ready to pick that up, right?"

Shan gave him a look that would kill. "How you gonna go from fuckin' me to immediately asking me about some business?"

"I gotta go baby, it's count time. You straight, right? Do I need to run everything down again?"

"No, Forever. I'm not a moron. Pick that shit up and when I leave dump the shit in the trash. That's not hard Forever." She rolled her eyes at him.

He smiled at her, then leaned over and gave her a kiss. "I'll see you tomorrow a'ight?" When she didn't answer he asked, "What's the matter?"

"Nothing," she lied as she watched him leave. Then said to herself, *I'm fucking somebody else's husband and don't even feel guilty. On top of that I'm getting ready to start movin' dope. What is happening to me?*

This was Shan's first experience with the dope game and she was nervous as hell. *If Peanut knew I was having anything to do with dope, he'd whip my ass!* She was talking to herself. *Oh, well. It's either he sit where he is or I do what I gotta do.*

Shan sat impatiently in the parking lot of the mini mart waiting on Silk to deliver the first package. Having spoke with her brother the night before he had tried to assure her that he was all right, but hearing the strain in his voice Shan realized that he wasn't all right and needed to get outta the spot that he was in.

"Stop crying, girl. You ain't in fifth grade no more. Your big bro is a'ight."

"But they beat you up and they . . . they . . . raped you," she cried.

"No they didn't. Who is telling you all this bullshit?"

"Brianna."

"Why you still fuckin' with that bitch? That hoe don't know

what the fuck she's talkin' about! Stay away from her, Shan. Do you hear what I'm saying?"

"I hear you."

"Do like I'm telling you. And stop all that damn crying."

"Okay boy, damn!" She wiped her eyes and blew her nose. "Your lawyer is supposed to call me tomorrow to set up a time for us to meet."

"I know you got me."

"I love you."

"I love you too."

"Be careful." Shan hung up and began crying again. She was really pissed at Brianna and them hoes that Peanut was fucking. One of them, CoCo, told her that Peanut didn't have any money over there but $3,300 dollars. When Shan told Peanut what she said he went off. The other one, Prissy, had almost $600. And Nick said he had eight grand but he never got back to her. He was officially MIA. When she went to collect from CoCo and Prissy they were nowhere to be found. So she wasn't depending on no one. Peanut had other funds but only he had access to them. But Shan wasn't sweatin' that. His lawyer needed 35,000 and she was gonna get it together by any means necessary.

When Shan had pulled into the mini mart, Silk was already across the street in his car waiting and watching her. His sister Tee Tee was in the front seat while he was on the phone. "Yo dawg, you should see this fine ass Shorty Forever got workin' for him! Um-Um-UMMumph! Damn man, Shorty is your type man, I'm tellin' you son. If I had a camera, I'd take a picture for you. If Forever ain't up in the joint smashin' that ass, tell him I said he stupid! I'ma ready to become an inmate up in that muthafucka!"

"Boy come on!" Tee Tee yelled. "I got things to do and Forever got a wife nigga! Plus, why would she want to fuck some nigga locked up?"

Silk ignored her as he kept on talking while starting the car. They headed for the mini mart across the street as he gave a description to whoever he was talking to of what Shan was wearing.

"Hang up Silk, Let's go!" When she went to grab the phone from him, he hung up.

Shan sat in the car with the door unlocked as instructed. Looking out of her rearview mirror she saw Silk and his sister approach her ride. Tee Tee hopped in the front, while Silk hopped in the back.

"Hey girl what's up?" Tee Tee said while slipping her the twenty-six hundred cash.

"Ain't nothing." Shan was cautiously looking from her to Silk in the rearview mirror. Silk was in the back on the passenger side taping the dope under the front seat.

"Yo, what's your name again?" He was sitting straight up and it didn't even look like he was doing anything but talking to her.

"Cindy."

"That's your real name?"

"Yup."

"A'ight then, Cindy. You good." And just as quick as him and Tee Tee jumped in the car, they jumped out.

Shan sat there dumbfounded as she watched Silk and Tee Tee get into their ride and pull off.

When she pulled up in front of her building she hurriedly grabbed the bag, jumped out the car and rushed inside to her apartment. She opened the bag, unwrapped the bundle, and there was a heavy shoe box taped up. She shook it and smelled it, then placed it back in the bag.

Okay. I'm a step closer to my goal, she said to herself. "I just got to get past Thursday's delivery." With that she decided to wind it down for the day. She fixed herself a nice tub of hot water and a glass of wine and called it a night.

Shan was sick of Brianna blowing up her two-way and her voice mail. She kept rambling on about Peanut holding her here and how he had stopped her from leaving. She even had mentioned that she thought about killing herself. Plus, she wanted to know if Shan read the letter that she mailed her. Shan never opened it. She didn't even bother to listen to all of her messages. *This bitch thinks that an apology is going to cut it and this will all blow over! She got me fucked up! I got something for her ass.* Shan thought to herself in disgust while clearing out her voice mail.

Twelve days, four deliveries later and constant sexin' between Forever and Shan, they were becoming quite comfortable with one another. Shan was bringing in whatever Forever wanted. Shan was even doing overtime, just to spend more time with Forever.

She was in her computer class seeing the last two students out when Forever stuck his head in the door.

"You want me to clean up in here tonight or wait until tomorrow?"

"Wait until tomorrow. I'm getting ready to lock up, but you can dump the trash and vacuum my floor before I go."

Forever smiled. "Is that all you want me to do?"

She disregarded his comment and she turned off the lights and locked the door. When they got to her office she said, "Forever I still need four thousand dollars. Baby, it's been almost two weeks," she pouted.

Bitches know how to work a nigga, he thought to himself. He sat down in her chair. "Come here." Shan did the opposite and sat down in the chair in front of her desk. "Come here, girl."

"Why I gotta beg Forever? I put in the work, I'm putting myself at risk, plus I'm fucking you. And on top of that I'm—"

"Hold up, hold up!" he cut her off. "You acting like I'm just using you. For a couple of weeks' worth of work I gave you what? Eight Gs? Come on now! Fair exchange ain't no robbery. I told you I got you. Now come here!"

"When?"

Forever laughed.

"It's not funny Forever. If it wasn't for my brother I wouldn't be doing none of this shit."

"Oh, so you just using me! That's what you telling me, right? My feelings are hurt now. Come here, I want you to use me right now." Forever was spoiled to the point of getting some pussy every time he saw her. And tonight before she got off work was going to be no different. Emptying the trash and vacuuming the floor would have to wait.

"Yo man, I didn't know what was taking you so long to check out this new honey dip. Forever got this shorty doin' the damn thang. He movin' more dope than niggas with a corner!" Silk as usual was talking nonstop as him and his main man waited for Shan to pull up. They were sitting in the car watching while Tee Tee and Danisha was in another car to make the drop. "Here she comes now yo!"

Briggen did a double take as he watched Shan park. "Ain't this a bitch!" He grabbed his cell phone and quickly dialed. "Tee Tee, cancel that for right now. I'll holla at you later."

"What's up dawg?" Silk was looking at Briggen with confusion. "What? Don't tell me you know Shorty?"

"A'ight, I won't then."

"Ahhhh dayum!! Didn't I tell you she was your type!! My nigga!! Am I the man, or what?" Silk was screaming and laughing at the same time. "It's about to go down!"

"Whatever man. Just wait until I get back." He got out and walked across the street to where Shan was. She was looking up at him, wondering why the fuck he was here, but at the same time she was shocked as hell. She couldn't even fix her mouth to speak. She hadn't seen Briggen since the day he got shot. Even though they had been talking over the phone she refused to see him.

"What? Cat got your tongue?" He snatched her car door open.

No . . . I . . . shit! . . . I'm just surprised to see you. The last time I saw you, you were lying over the top of me bleeding. Are you okay?"

"I'm not here to talk about that. What the fuck you think you're doing?"

"Close my door Calvin." She started her car up. He reached down, turned the ignition off and took the keys. "What do you want?"

"So what, you movin' dope now? And you fuckin' my little brother, Forever? You fuckin' him? That's my brother Shan!"

Shan's heart fell to her stomach. "Why are you worried about what I'm doing?" She didn't know what else to say.

He knew exactly what that meant. He gave her back her keys. "Go home Shan." And walked away.

Shan dialed Silk on the cell phone. She didn't know that he was right across the street. "Silk, where are you?"

"I'm right here. Ain't nothing jumpin' off tonight Shorty!"

"What you mean 'nothing'?" I'm supposed to be picking up some money!"

"You gotta talk to my man Briggen."

Shan jumped outta the car running to catch up with Briggen. "Why you hatin' Calvin? This is business!" she said through clenched teeth.

"Talk to Forever." He got in the car and left her standing there.

"Briggen wait! My brother . . . I need that money!" She watched them pull off and began to cry.

"Big bro, what's up?" Forever gave Briggen a warm brotherly hug. "Is everybody a'ight? Is Pops cool?" Forever began to get alarmed.

"Everybody's fine. How about you?" They both sat down.

"Everythang's everythang."

"Nyla and my niece okay?"

"Yeah. I know you know everything is gravy on my end. Nyla and Tameerah are fine. As a matter of fact, I thought you was her. She trippin' but it ain't nothing I can't handle. So what's up? I know you ain't come visit a nigga on lock to make small talk."

"You know that. Shan, what's up with you and her?"

"Shan?" Forever looked shocked. "You know her, man?"

"I fucked her a couple of times. I like her; I was hoping to put her in charge of one of my businesses."

"Fuck! What happened? I didn't know!"

"She came out to the club and ran into Sharia and Mia. They got to fightin' and shit. So she been pissed off at me ever since."

"Damn. Why you had her come around your crazy women?" Forever smirked, knowing how his brother was. "And where was Tami?" Forever was getting a kick outta this. Briggen had a ride and die bitch for each business that he ran, even his dope.

"I didn't invite her out. She just popped up. But back to you and her. I don't want her to get caught up in no shit. I need to use her. She's clean."

"Man it's too late now. All that shit we been moving is because of her."

"Shit man. Get another bitch. She ain't the only hoe working up in this piece."

"Man c'mon."

"Naw, you c'mon. I told you I was already fuckin' her. Now cut that shit off. Plus, I ain't giving her nothing else."

"Brig, you out there in the free world. There's a whole sea of clean bitches out there that you can get to run one of your businesses."

"I want to use her." Briggen got up, ready to go. He said what he had to say. "Why the fuck is she so pressed?"

"Her brother Peanut. She's tryna bail him out."

Briggen gave Forever a look that said I don't believe this shit. "Man you too reckless, you know that right? Don't get her caught up man. Clean that shit up."

"I got this bruh." Forever got up and gave his brother another hug.

20

SHADEE AND BRIANNA

Brianna turned towards the clock and it was almost eleven. She hesitated before dialing Shadee's cell phone. She needed some money.

"Hello," Janay answered. "Hello."

"I need to speak to Shadee." Brianna finally said.

"Who is this?"

"Is he there? This is Brianna."

Click. Janay hung up on her.

"Bitch!" Brianna spat as she redialed. After five rings his voice mail kicked in. "Shadee this is an emergency. Call me." She clicked off and dialed his house phone.

"What's up?" He finally answered.

"Hey. It's me. You got company?"

After he woke up a little he asked, "B, what's good?"

"I need a favor. Can you come over now?"

"I'm still in the bed, B. What's up?"

"I need some money and it is an emergency. If it wasn't, you know I wouldn't be asking."

Shadee laughed. "Girl, you a trip. Why you ain't got no money?"

"I got money but not the amount that I need. Can't you come over? I can't talk over the phone."

"You can come over here."

"You got company don't you?"

"Naw girl. I told you I'm asleep. Well, I was until you called."

"I just called your cell phone and that bitch hung up on me."

Shadee looked on his nightstand, then picked up his jeans from off the floor. "Damn," he mumbled when he realized he didn't have it. "You can come over."

"Okay I'll be there."

Shadee dialed Janay on his cell phone. When the voice mail kicked in, he yelled, "Fuck!" He then dialed her house phone.

"What?" she spat.

"Why you answering the phone like that? What's the matter with you?"

"Shadee, don't start with me."

"I'm not startin' shit. You need to chill the fuck out! I need you to drop off my cell phone." Then warned, "And stop answerin' it!"

"Nigga please. I haven't touched your phone."

"Stop lying girl. Brianna told me she just called and you hung up on her."

"You know I never liked that gold diggin' hoe. All she do is use you. She don't got no love for you."

Shadee laughed. "Baby, payback is a mutha. Just as good as bustin' a nut."

"What is that supposed to mean?"

"Nothing. I was just thinking out loud."

Janay was quiet as she thought about what he just said. Then when it dawned on her she yelled, "Shadee, I know you ain't gonna do that girl like that!" She was pacing back and forth. "Sha! Answer me! You ain't gonna do that girl like that, are you?"

"Bring my phone over. I'll see you later." *Click.*

On Brianna's way out the door Skye was coming up the stairs. "I almost missed you huh?" He was flashing that million dollar sexy smile.

"I'm on my way out." She shut the door behind her. "What's up?"

"Open the door. I need to holla at you."

Brianna rolled her eyes but did as she was told. As soon as the door closed he pulled her close and began kissing her neck.

"I'm running late Skye." She tried to squirm away.

"Who else you got for me?"

She sucked her teeth. "Can we discuss this another time?"

"No, we can't. Who else you got? What up with that nigga Shadee?"

She snapped her neck back. "Ain't nothing happenin' with him!"

Skye smiled. "You said that a little too damn quick with too much emotion. How you know ain't nothin' happenin'?"

"Because I know."

"Let me find out you done caught feelings for this nigga."

This nigga must be smokin' something. She said to herself. "Let me see what else I come up with."

"Naw baby. I want the man himself. Shadee. Where does he live?"

"I don't know that. He always comes over here. Just like you do."

"You been fuckin' this nigga for how long? And you don't know where he lives? Bullshit!"

"I don't know where you live. Do I?"

Skye sighed in exasperation. "A'ight look. This is how we gonna do this. I. Want. Shadee."

"I'm not gonna. Give. You. Shadee."

As soon as those words left her mouth she felt Skye's hands around her neck.

"Like I said, this is what you're gonna do. You get me his address and I need to know when and where is his next move." He let her neck go. "Are we clear?"

"You can't make me set him up Skye."

"Oh, you're gonna bring him to me," he threatened.

"And if I don't?"

"Ask your mom and sister what time it is."

"What?" Brianna's heart fell to her feet. She pushed him with all of her strength, causing him to fall back onto the couch. "Nigga, what did you say?"

Skye just sat there smiling at her. Finally he said, "Come here and suck my dick before you go."

"You better leave my family outta this!" She was so pissed that she started crying.

"Oh, so you do have a heart?" He got up, grabbed her, giving her a bear hug. "Girl stop crying. Just help me out and everything will be a'ight."

"Get off me nigga! You ain't right. You know you ain't right." She pushed him away before wiping her face and grabbing her bag. "You already got me in enough trouble. I'm late."

"Hold up! Hold up! You can't break me off a quickie?" She ignored him and opened the door. He was thinking about making her suck his dick but changed his mind. "So it's like that?" He leaned over and kissed her on the cheek. "A'ight. So I guess that means we got an understanding. Cool. I'm out!"

She watched him go back down the stairs. She was devastated and felt as if her world was coming down all around her. First Peanut and Shan, now her mother and sister. She could handle herself but getting her family involved was a whole 'nother ball game. She still did not want any harm to come to them. The last time she spoke to her sister was a few months before she went to prison. Her sister found out that Brianna had fucked her husband. It had been even longer since she had spoke to her mother. She was mad at her because she felt that her own daughter was the one responsible for her boyfriend, Alston, doing twelve years for sexual assault. Even though she was not on speaking terms with either one of them, she still did not want any harm to come to them.

After she got herself together she jumped into her Lexus and headed for Shadee's, not knowing what to do. She got with Skye thinking that he was a lick and she ended up being the lick. She didn't even see it or him coming.

When she pulled up in Shadee's driveway, she sat a few minutes, still trying to get herself together. She decided against telling him what Skye wanted her to do, at least for now.

She rang the doorbell for what seemed like an eternity. When Shadee finally opened the door she was like, "fuck it!" and was just about to leave and was all the way down the stairs.

Sha was wet, with a towel wrapped around his waist. "I know you wasn't tryna leave, after you done got me outta my deep sleep."

She came back up the stairs. "You knew I was on my way over, why you gonna jump in the shower?" She placed her hand on his flat abs and gently pushed him aside. She was trying her best to act like everything was just fine.

"I wanted to be fresh and clean for when you got here." He looked at her ass filling up her hip huggers. "What nigga done pissed you off?"

"Why does it have to be a nigga? Why can't it be a hoe?"

"Well I know something got you tensed up. Come here." He grabbed her arm and pulled her to him.

He pulled the towel from around his waist and popped her on the behind.

"Stop playing, that shit hurts!"

"Well come dry me off then."

She sucked her teeth but came over and snatched the towel from him. He reached over and grabbed two handfuls of that ass, squeezing it before getting him some tongue. She then ran the towel over his arms, chest, and abs.

"You already dried off on my damn clothes!"

Shadee stood there looking Brianna up and down. Finally he told her, "You're so fine." Then asked, "You think that's one of my weaknesses? Why I'm so weak for you? Why I let you get away with so much shit? And over and over I let you fuck me over. What do you think B?" He walked away and headed to the bathroom. She followed behind him in silence. "Of course I'm not gonna get an answer to that. So, go ahead and tell Daddy what you done got yourself into this time." He grabbed his electric razor and began fumbling with it.

"I need some money," she ashamedly answered.

"I know you need money, but why the urgency?" He was taking the electric shaver apart and purposely cut himself. "Fuck!" he yelled, watching the blood drip down his index finger.

She went over to the sink where he stood. "Listen to you. Daddy got a baby cut on his finger and now he's crying," she teased.

He put his finger to her mouth. "Here, make it better." He laced her bottom lip with blood before forcing his finger inside her mouth. She dutifully and seductively sucked the death warrant off of his fingers while he watched. When he was satisfied he pulled her close and began undressing her. "Damn, baby. What you do, paint these on?" He struggled with her hip huggers. "Damn!" He laughed as he finally got them down.

"I thought you said you liked me in this outfit," she purred as she dropped to her knees and immediately put him in her mouth. He grabbed her head with both hands and moaned as she worked her magic. She didn't let up until the veins on his dick looked like they were gonna explode and he was harder than Chinese arithmetic. She then leaned back and smiled at her handiwork.

He glanced down at her. "Oh, so you think you did something?"

"Nigga, you know I did. Listen at you. You can hardly talk. Plus, look how thick and hard you are." She had stood up and was seductively rolling down her thong. As soon as she pulled them off he grabbed her by her hair.

"Finish me off." And gently pushed her down to her knees again.

She licked, sucked and teased the head until she thought it was gonna puke. Then went to licking and sucking on his balls. When she eased a finger up inside his ass he said, "B! Hold up! Hold up!"

She smiled up at him. "Aw, nigga, you know you bout it, bout it!" she said, but was only joking.

He grabbed her this time with force by her hair and pulled her up.

"Oowww, Sha! I was only playin'."

He pushed her over to the sink. "Wash your hands." And he stormed outta the bathroom.

When she came into the bedroom he was pacing back and forth. She laid down on the bed, spread her legs and started playing with her pussy.

"Sha, come here Daddy. I'm sorry. I was only tryna finish you off like you said. I was gonna make you come reeeaal hard and looong. Make you remember why you can't leave me alone." She put one hand on her breast and was grinding on her fingers. "Now come here and remind me why I just can't stop fucking with *you*. Come here Daddy. You know you like the smell and the taste of this pussy. I know you ain't gonna make me cum by myself," she moaned.

That got his attention. He came over to the bed and crawled between her legs. She placed her hand on top of his head and motioned for him to go downtown. He ignored her, removing her hand and plunged deep inside her.

"Sha you don't have on a condom!" He was already grindin'. "Baby!" she called out. He threw one of her legs over his shoulder and started fuckin' the pussy like he was mad at it. "Sha, slow down," she pleaded. When he felt like finally slowing down he did. "Thank you." She moaned as she matched her rhythm with his. "What's. The matter. With. You?" Their rhythm flowed like the motion in the ocean. "Oh, right. There, that's. My. Spot. Sha, I'm cumming!" She screamed as her body shook, quivered, then fell limp. He pulled out and flipped her over onto her stomach, slowly kissing her from her neck, traveling down to her spine. He spread her ass cheeks and started licking her crack. "Ooh faster,

Sha. Faster." He moaned and licked then fucked her in the ass until he was ready to turn her over and eat her pussy. She came instantly. He lay sprawled out on his back, looking at his dick standing straight up and slowly swaying side to side.

He grabbed her by her hair and pulled her downward. He didn't have to tell her what time it was. She automatically took him into her mouth deep throating his dick until he was hollering like a bitch.

"Briannaaaaa." Was his last word before he came and released in her mouth, what felt like buckets of cum. Then he went limp. They lay there, each lost in their own train of thought, undisturbed and perfectly still until the doorbell rang.

"Who are you expecting?" Brianna rolled over.

"No one that I know of." Shadee got up and went to the door, yelling "Who is it?" Forgetting that he had told Janay to drop off his cell phone.

"It's me. Who was you expectin'?" She had just pulled out her key, not wanting to walk in on him and get another shocker.

He unlocked the door and let her in. "What brings you over this way?"

She looked at his naked body up and down, thinking to herself he don't even look like he has the virus. "I'm scared to ask who you got up in here."

"What's up Janay?" Sha asked her.

"They found Biz's body." She whispered. "I thought everything would be taken care of."

"Did anyone come and question you?"

"No."

"Well then. Don't even worry about it. I already told you, you straight Janay. Now anything else?"

"Oh, now my man is putting me out?" She threw his cell phone at him, just missing his head.

"Your man?" Brianna walked up and put her arm around his waist.

Janay started laughing. Even though Sha could see that she was hurt. "Keeping your enemies close aren't we?" She smirked at Brianna.

"What's that 'sposed to mean? Sha what's with this hood rat ass bitch?"

"Bitch I don't have to spell it out."

"Hoe, I'm not talking to you." Brianna flipped her the bird.

"Sha, put this bitch ass hoe in check before I do."

"B, let me holla at Janay."

Brianna sucked her teeth and rolled her eyes at Janay before giving Shadee some tongue.

"Bitch, please. You know what?" Janay placed both of her hands around her own neck and began making choking noises, wheezing and making her eyes bulge.

"Excuse us." He slapped Brianna on the ass and watched her walk away.

"Real funny Janay." He said, punching her in the mouth, causing blood to gush out of her bottom lip. "Don't fuck with me."

"You hit me!" she gasped.

Swinging at him, he ducked, then put her in a choke hold. "Now what? Girl what's the matter with you?" She was crying but no sounds were coming out. He turned her loose yelling, "What is the matter with you? Huh?"

"Everything Shadee! But you gonna hit me over that skank ass hoe?" She stormed to the door, turned around and said, "You gonna choose that hoe over me? It's like that between us? That hurts Shadee. But you know what? I can't be mad because y'all deserve each other."

"It's not like that Janay."

"Fuck you Shadee. Because you're gonna need me and our son before we need you!" She slammed the door so hard one of the pictures of him and her slid down the wall.

"Janay!" He ran to the door after her. "Janay!" She jumped in her car and pulled off.

"Damn!" he cursed as he slammed the door.

"Sha what was that all about?"

He brushed past her and went to the bedroom. She was right on his heels. "What was that about?"

"Nothing B. How much you need?" He asked as he was throwing on some clothes.

"I need 20Gs. What was she talking about?" She went back to it.

"I don't have that much here."

She sucked her teeth. "What do you have?"

"Let me check. Get dressed. I gotta run."

"I need a shower."

"You don't have time. Get dressed, I gotta go."

"What? You gotta run after that bitch?"

"Get dressed. And when did you start caring who the fuck I ran after?" He went in the closet and when he came back he handed her some money.

She thumbed through it. "Two Gs? Sha come on. I'm in a bind."

Sha wanted to make her sweat. "That's all I got B," he lied. He was now dressed and ready to go. He went into the bathroom and gathered up her clothes. When he turned around she was right behind him. "Get dressed. I gotta go."

She snatched them from him and stormed into the bedroom. "I need more than this!"

He stood there with his keys in hand. "C'mon. Let's go."

A week later . . .

"Yo B. I'm coming over. Just making sure you home."

"Where you been? I've been trying to get in touch with you." Brianna sounded a little tipsy.

"I was outta town. What? You wanted to know where I was going so you could set me up again?" He decided to make fun of her but keep it real at the same time.

"That ain't me no more Shadee. And you don't know how sorry I am for doing you like that."

Shadee held the phone out and looked at it as if it were a snake. This didn't sound like the scandalous, gold diggin' Brianna that he had grown use to. However, her change in attitude wasn't gonna stop him from giving her the ultimate dose of payback.

"Are you there Sha?"

"Yeah I'm here. I'll be there in a few."

Shadee had needed to get away. Mainly from Janay. He still couldn't believe that Janay had found him out, discovering his secret life. Talkin' about a nigga being embarrassed! He almost shit on himself. He was still beating himself up for getting lax. He shouldn't have fucked Doc in Janay's crib. Rule number one. He didn't know what the fuck had come over him. Hell, he thought that she was gone to her mom's crib. He wanted to kill Doc for acting like a straight-up bitch, whining and all that shit that bitches do. That's what blew the lid off his cover, he convinced himself. That shit there really threw him for a loop. It was almost as if Doc was gettin' off on the shit. Any other time they would just fuck and keep it moving. No conversation. No lovey-dovey shit. That shit was for faggots. He couldn't understand why Doc was acting like Monica—"So Gone." Blowing up his voice mail, keying his ride, parking in front of the crib, just plain stalking him. Last night Shadee had to threaten him and tell him if he didn't cut the bullshit he was going to cut off his dick and stuff it in his ass. He told him niggas don't act the way he's been acting: like a bitch! The only bright side was that he knew his secret was safe with Janay. Especially since she got them bodies. She didn't want to go to jail for murder. She had been blowin' up his two-way but he didn't care. She was the last person he wanted to see. He was still very embarrassed in front of her.

He took his time and drove to South Carolina to see his pop. He had wanted to clear his mind and confide in him but couldn't bring himself to do it. His pops loved Janay. While he was down there he visited his mother who was in a nursing home battling Alzheimer's. So he couldn't talk to her either. And now the demons were festering inside and he felt like he was going crazy! Being on the DL was going with him to his grave.

The only thing that was presently on his mind was getting Brianna back. Shadee began to reminisce as he put his ride on cruise control.

The two of them went back to elementary. They use to live across the hall from each other in the same building. Their mothers made them go to church together on Sundays; they walked to and from school together every day; Shadee always had her back—they even went to their ninth grade prom together. Even though they went their separate ways after that, they never went far and the bond that they built during childhood was never broken. Shadee did his thing and Brianna did hers. He had never looked at her sexually until her twentieth birthday. She was hooked up with this baller named Black Jax. He should have been called Black Ugly Jax because that's what he was: black and ugly. As a matter of fact, he's the reason why she ended up having to do that fed bid. Brianna was a money lover. She didn't care who had it or how they got it!

Black Jax had Club Steez on lock for a double birthday bash. Brianna and Jax were born hours apart. She came through at 10:00 P.M. and he came through at 12:14 A.M. the next day. Shadee had found out by word of mouth that the party was going down.

He had just come home from doing eleven months on a possessions charge. He was sitting at the bar looking around, trying to decide who he was going to take home. The girl sitting next to him who was buying him drinks was talking too much. However, she was fine and appeared to have money. He was the male version of Brianna. He got his own money but at the same time, when a hoe wanted to get with him she had to have hers.

His eyes zoomed in on Brianna. He hadn't seen her in over a year. She had on a white halter top and a white miniskirt to match. *Damn! Look at my girl! She lookin' good!* The thigh high stockings and garter belt was really throwin' him for a loop.

The young lady sitting next to him looked at him and snapped back her neck as if to say "No, this nigga ain't disrespectin' me like this!"

Shadee ignored her as he watched Black Jax politic as if he were the president, thinkin' he was the shit while wearing Brianna on his arm. Even though he had to admit that while he was down and from what he heard in the few hours that he was home, Black Jax was that nigga. Shadee needed a come-up and it looked like Brianna had his ticket.

When he saw Black Jax kiss her on the cheek, then step off with a couple of his boys, Shadee eased off the bar stool and headed her way. She was now talking to a group of ladies when all of a sudden they turned their attention to him. When Brianna saw that it was him she screamed, "Sha, is that you?" Practically jumping in his arms and breaking his neck. "When did you get home?" She stepped back to get a good look at him. "Damn, you look good! Look at you, all buff and shit! Let me find out that's all you been doing with your time. Did your moms give you the money I gave her to send you?"

"Yeah she sent it."

"Sha," she whined, giving him another hug. "When did you get home?"

"Day before yesterday."

"Why you ain't come over?"

"Girl I don't even know where you live anymore."

"You could have asked your moms; she has all of my info." She still had her arms around his neck.

"You been a'ight?" *Damn, she smells good. And she feels so soft.*

"Yeah I'm fine."

"I can see that. You lookin' scrumptious." He ran his hands over her ass. "What you doin' with that busta ass nigga?"

"Sha you know I gots to get mines. I gots to live. That's all that's up."

"Well I need to get mines. What's up?"

"Just say the word babee. I'm down for whatever. You know that you family and ain't nothin' changed."

"Good as you lookin' I don't wanna be family no more." He had pulled her close.

Brianna surprised, smiled as she pressed up against his dick. "You need to ask me to dance or something before folks get to talking." She didn't want to let him go.

"You want to dance?"

"Sure. After all, it is my birthday." She grabbed his hand and pulled him onto the dance floor.

"Who is that?" One of the girls in the circle Brianna had just left wanted to know.

"Ain't no telling," Patrice answered. "She better hope Black Jax don't catch her dancin' all up on that nigga like that."

Sure enough, as they watched, Brianna and Shadee was all over one another as if they were long-lost lovers. "How long you been gone Sha?"

"Eleven months."

"Damn. Who the lucky hoe?"

Sha blushed. "What you mean?"

"You know what I mean nigga! Some lucky hoe got her back banged out by a nigga who ain't had no pussy in eleven months. Who is she?"

"Why? What you tryna say?"

"Nigga you hear me loud and clear. I wish it was me. That's what I'm saying."

"Yeah, well, it's goin' down tonight."

"Boy please. You know it done already went down! You forgot who you talkin' to, so stop playin'."

"I ain't playin', Ma. That honey dip sittin' at the bar rollin' her eyes at you, she gonna get all this."

Brianna fell into his trap as she craned her neck over his shoulder to see who he was talking about. "Nigga, please!" she snapped when she saw that she was no competition. "Fuck that hoe! You got a pro right here!"

Shadee laughed at her wisecrack. "How you gonna break away from that nigga? Look like you all claimed up and he clockin' your every move. I see that as a little problem because foreal, foreal, I wanna fuck you now while you got these pretty ass stockings on and no panties. These shits is sexy as hell," he said as he rubbed up and down her thigh.

"Nigga you ain't said nothin' but a word. In about fifteen minutes meet me in front of the ladies' room upstairs." She gave him a wicked grin.

"Bet." Here, scandalous ass Brianna was planning on fucking another nigga in the club while her man was only a few feet away.

Damn. Brianna said to herself while looking at the Cartier on her wrist.

Twenty minutes had passed and Black Jax was drunk and not letting Brianna out of his sight. Jax and her had been kickin' it for over a year. He was ballin' outta control, took damn good care of her but was jealous as hell and a terrible fuck. He was so bad that Brianna was desperate enough to fuck Shadee, who was really like family. On top of that, with so many folks around she was still willing to take a chance of getting busted by anyone, including Jax.

"Jax baby, my stomach feels funny. I'll be back. Let me go to the bathroom," she whispered into his ear.

"What?" he yelled at her as he threw back a straight shot of Henny.

"My stomach feels funny. Let me go to the ladies' room."

"I ain't stoppin' you! But don't make me come lookin' for your ass!"

"Now why would you have to do that?" She kissed him on the cheek as she eased away from their table. "Damn!" She mumbled as she began pushing her way through the crowd, hoping that Shadee was where she told him to be because fifteen minutes had come and gone. "Happy Birthday, girl!" Her cousin Mingo had grabbed her and was hugging her so tight she could barely breathe. "Thanks Mingo. I'll talk to you later."

"Oh, okay girl. You wearin' that outfit."

"I know." Brianna said. "Jealous bitches," she mumbled, finally making it to the steps. When she got to the top of the stairs her pussy was so wet the juice was oozing down her thighs. She looked towards the ladies' restroom and Shadee was there but he wasn't alone. Some chick with what looked like a pair of double Ds that were too big for her body was all up in his face. "Sha I was lookin' all over for you!" She grabbed him around his waist pulling him away from double D. Double D was standing there waiting and expecting Shadee to say something.

When he didn't she said to Brianna, "You are so rude!"

"Excuse us. I'll holla at you." Shadee told her and watched her ass jiggle when she turned around and walked away pissed.

Brianna sucked her teeth as she pulled him down the hall. "Nigga you can do betta than that."

"I was getting ready to bounce. I thought you ain't want to get with this."

There was a line outside of both bathrooms. So Brianna pulled him up another set of stairs which led to an attic door that was locked. "Aw dayum."

"Fuck it!" Shadee said as he ran his hand up her thigh, not giving her a chance to turn around, and began fingering her pussy. Smiling at how wet she was he immediately pulled his dick out and hit it from the back.

The next day he went to her house and hit it again. The day after that she snuck out and went to a hotel and got it again. However, it didn't take long for them to agree that they were too much alike to be a couple. But just like Peanut, Shadee was someone who could get it any time. But the bond of growing up together wouldn't allow things to stop there. She did eventually set up Black Jax and that's how Shadee got his come up, once again.

So now here he was, back from South Carolina and at her front door. The bond that they had had over the years was broken in half when she set him up and almost got him killed. Over the years he had been nothing but good to her. He cared for her almost as much as he cared for Janay. This bitch had to be taught that the line had to be drawn somewhere. Now the only thing on his mind was killing her: slowly.

When Brianna opened the door and saw it was him, she gave him a big hug. She immediately began to vent. Telling him how Peanut knocked her in the mouth and how scared she was of him and how she thinks he put a hit out on Nick, destroying her plans of relocating and starting her life over. She told him about Shan still not speaking to her, nor were her mother or her sister. She cried telling him how she was all alone and now she knew the meaning of a cold, cold world.

He listened intently as she poured her heart out. He assured her everything would be all right and that he was there for her like always. He assured her that nothing had changed between them.

After that and for the next few days, before he would come see Brianna he would first fuck a nigga in the ass, wouldn't wash his dick and would come over and fuck Brianna in every hole on her body. Unprotected.

21

FOREVER

"Damn man!" Zeke buried his head up under his pillow. Forever kept kicking on his cell bars. "Get up, man. I need to holla at you."

Zeke raised up to snatch his alarm clock off the chair. "Man, it's only quarter to twelve, my bunkie ain't here, so let me enjoy this moment. Why ain't your ass on the visit instead of trying to stop me from getting my beauty rest?"

"Man, Nyla is trippin'. I got the feeling she creepin'! And I did get a visit . . . from my brother."

That got Zeke's full attention. "What! Big bad Briggen graced the prison house visiting room! Awwww shieeiit! Sumthin' goin' down!" Zeke got outta the bed, took a piss, washed his face and brushed his teeth. He could see that Forever was truly pissed off.

When Forever caught Zeke staring at him he yelled, "What the fuck you lookin' at? Come on, nigga!"

"Man, get your panties out your ass! I ain't do shit to ya! And if you want to vent on me, yo ass gonna have to wait until I'm damn good and ready!"

"Whatever, yo. Meet me outside! Slow motherfucker!" Forever

hissed as he stormed away. *Beauty rest?* He had to laugh at that one.

Zeke shook his head at his boy. After he threw on some sweats he rushed out to see what was up with Forever. When he got outside Forever was standing there waiting on him. "Bout time!" Forever said as they hit the track with Forever wasting no time filling Zeke in. "Man." Forever started laughing. "You ain't gonna believe this shit!" He started laughing again. "Brig and Shan use to fuck!" He looked at Zeke, anticipating his response. When he didn't get the response he was expecting he yelled, "Did you hear me?"

"Yeah nigga, I heard you. I'm just waitin' to hear the rest. I know y'all ain't gonna let some pussy halt the business. Pimp, I told you; them hoes come a dime a dozen."

"Well you need to tell Brig that because that nigga all in his feelings over one bitch, when you and me both know that the nigga got a dozen."

"You should have punched that nigga in the nose! Big brother and all!"

Zeke was clearly pissed off. He wasn't tryna see his dollars fly out the window, especially over some pussy.

"Well the nigga told me to find somebody else because he ain't giving that bitch nothing else."

"Man that's fucked up! Tell him I said so too. I can't believe this shit! He willin' to stick you and himself for the paper? And over a hoe! What part of the game is this shit?" Zeke said, goin' off.

"Shan ain't come to work Thursday or Friday. I don't know what he said to her. She might come in today or tomorrow. So playa, our backs are up against the wall right now. We either, (a) wait till we find somebody else and keep using Brig. Or (b) keep using Shan but use the competition, Skinny Pimp, and piss Brig the fuck off."

"What the fuck he want us to do Ever? We both got families to feed. And I know that nigga know firsthand that it cost money to live in prison." Frustrated, Zeke said, "Whatever man! It's on you. I ain't gonna come between you and your brother. However you wanna do it, let's do it. I ain't got shit else to say."

"Man you already said what you had to say. So let me see where Shan's head is at and then I'll let you know."

"Whatever, man." Zeke was still pissed.

"Now peep this shit. I called Nyla last night all the way until they cut the phones off. Then this morning at 6:30, I finally catch her. I said 'Damn, you had me worried as fuck!' Come to find out her ass was out running the streets. I went the fuck off!"

"Man how many times I told you, you can't have complete control. You up in here nigga! When you gonna accept that? So what she went out? It ain't like she goes out all the time. Hell, she don't hardly go out at all!"

"That ain't the point man."

"Then what is the point?"

Forever was quiet. Not knowing what his point was other than the fact that he was selfish, didn't want to lose Nyla and scared that if she started to run the streets some other nigga would snatch her up. Especially since she had been talking about how tired she was of this jail shit. The devil was playing tricks with his mind. He was now getting paranoid. So they ended up arguing back and forth over the phone. She hung up on him and didn't even show up on the visit. This was the first time she ever pulled a stunt like this. His gut was telling him that she had someone else. So Forever was really fucked up about the whole situation.

"Forever," Zeke broke his train of thought. "Chill out, man. She went out last night. It's over. If I was you and Nyla was my woman, I'd call her up to apologize and beg her to come on the visit tomorrow. She works hard man. She's a good woman. You better not let your insecurities push her away. You can't control shit in here. You listening to me?"

"I hear you."

"A'ight man. I gotta check on our shit." Zeke gave him dap and left Forever outside. An hour and a half later Forever went to the phone and called Nyla.

Shan didn't come to work Saturday or Sunday. When she finally showed up on Monday, Forever was pissed to the nth degree, as he hung around the Education Department waiting on her. He looked at his watch; she was almost an hour late and in twenty more minutes he had an appointment to get his knee x-rayed.

"Damn girl, I thought you went into hiding or some shit like that." Forever smirked as she unlocked her door.

"I'm off on weekends. I thought you knew that."

"How you gonna take off knowing that I'm here?"

"Please. That's why I'm in the predicament I'm in now. Coming to see you."

"I got an appointment to get my knee x-rayed but I'll be back. We got a lotta shit to discuss."

"Yeah, we sure do. I'm anxious to see how you respond to what I got to talk about."

"I already know what you got to talk about."

"Oh no. I don't think so playa." And she slammed the door in Forever's face, hoping that he wasn't gonna respond to her the way her intuition was telling her he would.

Forever plopped in his usual seat in front of her desk. He looked Shan over. She looked tired and stressed.

"You a'ight? Why you haven't been to see me? You had me worried about you."

Shan leaned forward onto her desk looking Forever straight in the eyes. "Where do you want me to start? Oh I forgot, it's all about your paper, so I might as well let you say what you gotta say first."

Forever leaned back. "What's that supposed to mean?"

"Just say what you gotta say Forever. You wanna know if I was fuckin' your brother? To answer the question, yeah, I did once. And now, since he thinks that me and you are fucking he's pissed off. The other night he wouldn't give me the package or the four thousand dollars that you know I need. He told me I needed to talk to you. And on top of that"—she grabbed her purse, pulled out a plastic bag and threw it at him.

"What's this?" He examined it as if it was lethal.

"A pregnancy test Forever! Pink means positive. Blue means negative." She glared at him, anticipating a response.

Forever caught a lump in his throat and threw the plastic bag back at her. "I know you ain't telling me what I'm thinking you are?"

"Telling you Forever? I'm showing you! What? You want me to say it? I'm pregnant! You want me to spell it out? I'm P-R-E-G-N-A-N-T!"

Forever just stared at her, waiting for her to say she's joking or something. When she didn't he leaned forward, smothering his face in his hands. "Shit! How the fuck?"

"I'm keepin' it Forever," she interrupted him.

He looked up with the quickness. "You what?"

"I'm keeping it."

Forever sighed. "Shan. What the fuck you talking about? Do you hear yourself? You remember who I am? A nigga in prison with a wife. I don't think you want to do that. You can't do that!"

"What? Oh so now you want to all of a sudden be this responsible and logical family man? What are you saying Forever? Go ahead; I want to hear you say it! Tell me to get an abortion!" she was screaming.

"Lower your voice man."

"Fuck my voice! Go ahead and say it! Tell me to get an abortion! You say it and I swear I will fuck you up!" she threatened.

"What's that suppose to mean? Do you hear yourself? You know we was just fucking. Mixing business with pleasure."

"Nigga, no, you didn't just say that!"

"Come on Shan. You was fucking to get what you wanted and I was fucking you to get what I wanted. But you gotta get rid of it. Let's keep it real now."

The tears were rolling down her cheeks. *I'm glad he didn't disrespect by asking me how do I know if the baby was mine.* That was the only relief she felt. Shan's voice trembled as she said, "Well nigga, we now got us a baby on the way, and that's keeping it real!"

The next day Forever went to sick call and got an idle for the rest of the week. He didn't want to deal with Shan at all until he figured out what he was going to do. This pregnancy shit had him stressing like a mutha. Zeke was on him because all of the dope was gone and the customers were feinin'. Forever calmly told him, "Zeke man, we ain't starvin'. So business will have to be put on hold for a minute."

Forever had finally smoothed everything over with Nyla. He apologized and the whole nine yards. As they were sitting in the visiting hall, Forever looked up and in comes Shan. When she finally made eye contact with Forever, he gave her a look that said, "Bitch don't even think about it." And just to be sure he looked at Nyla and said, "Excuse me baby, let me go take a leak." He went over to the desk where the officer's station was.

"What's up Thompson?" Officer Mendez was one of the cool visiting room officers.

"Let me out. I need to go to the restroom." He then turned to Shan and said, "What's up boss? I see you decided to come back to work."

Shan came over to where he was. "Make sure you're in my office before I leave today." And walked away.

When Forever came back from the restroom Nyla shot at him, "What was that all about?"

"What?"

"Forever don't play dumb. Who is the broad?"

"She works in education."

"And?" Her left eyebrow raised up.

"And what Nyla?"

She stared at him, and it felt like forever to Forever. Her eyes felt as if they were piercing through his soul. She finally spoke. "Okay Forever. Don't say I didn't give you a chance to come clean," she snapped.

"Come clean? What is you talkin' about?"

"I gave you a chance Forever. And that's all I'm going to say."

Damn. Forever said to himself. *Shit seems to be crumbling all around me.*

By the time the visit was over Forever was all tensed up. Then, on top of that, Shan came back into the visiting room, throwing daggers at him, which only made Nyla that much more suspicious. Then when he walked past the TV room both TVs were showing a video of Usher revealing his "Confessions." When he grabbed his Walkman to run off some of the tension he was feeling, there was Usher again revealing his "Confessions."

He remembered that Shan wanted to see him but he was not in the mood for any conversation from her, even though getting between her thighs would surely ease all of the tension he was feeling. But he didn't have together what his next move was gonna be. "Fuck it," he said out loud. "I'll see her when I see her." And he went outside to run. He needed to clear his head.

Monday afternoon Forever made it into work. Shan cut into his ass as soon as he stepped foot into her office.

"I waited for you Forever. I told you I needed to talk to you."

"No you didn't, you just told me to be in your office."

Shan sucked her teeth. "I—"

He cut her off. "Shan I'm here now. I had to get my head together. So talk."

"You had to get your head together? What about me? I'm the one pregnant! I'm the one needing money! You said you got your head together, so what's up Forever? If you gonna leave me hanging let me know now." Her voice was trembling but she refused to cry.

"A'ight, look. We can keep getting money together. My brother ain't gonna fuck with you so I gotta set you up with some new folks."

"How soon?"

"By the end of the week. A'ight?"

She sucked her teeth. "And that's it? That's all you got to say?" Shan jumped up and smacked him dead across the face.

Forever, on instinct, grabbed her by her throat. "What the fu—"

"Tap Tap." Forever turned to look at the door, then he pushed Shan back down into her chair. She gagged a little, rubbed her neck and said, "Come in." When the inmate came in Forever walked out. "Mr. Thompson, I am not through with you." She then looked at the young man and said, "Come back in about an hour please and go tell Thompson I said to come in here now. His work is not finished."

"Yes ma'am." The inmate turned back around and left out. *What the fuck?*

When Forever came back in he calmly said, "What?" But she could tell that he was pissed off.

"What? I'm pregnant that's what!" She was pacing back and forth pulling on her locks. "Bear with me for a minute Forever. I guess I'm having a hard time accepting that what we've been doing don't mean shit to you. Close my fuckin' door Forever! I'm usually a good judge of character," she continued, "but I'm having a hard time accepting that you don't feel shit for me. I can't believe my judgment about you was all wrong Forever."

"Look. I need you to consider an abortion. I told you before, you know I got a family. But me and you, from this point on, can only do business. In a couple of days let me know what you want to do about the baby."

Shan snapped. "Get out Forever!" she screamed. "Get the fuck out!" She picked up her coffee mug and threw it at him.

On her way home she pulled over at a CK's and ordered a cup

of tea. Finding a booth in the corner she slumped down in the seat. *Damn, I need to talk to Peanut.* She swiftly wiped the tears off her face. *I'm transporting drugs, putting my freedom on the line. I'm pregnant by a married man who's in prison. What the fuck? That bitch Brianna! All this shit is her fault. I hate her!*

22

BRIANNA AND SHADEE

Even though Shadee had been over Brianna's for the last week she still was lonely and missed the companionship of her girl, Shan. But right now she was on cloud nine because last night Shadee had proposed to her. His proposal really threw her for a loop. There were rose petals sprinkled over the table that was draped with fine Irish linen set with Tiffany Platinum china and Baccarat crystal goblets. There was filet mignon, lobster tails with drawn butter, baked potatoes and asparagus. For dessert they had cheesecake smothered in fresh strawberries. He had set the table himself. The candlelight shimmered and sparkled as he threw on a slow jamz wedding CD and then popped the question. Of course Brianna didn't hesitate in accepting. She was dying to tell Shan the news but kept getting her voice mail.

The following morning Shadee got up early to go take care of some business. Brianna decided to use this time to get some housecleaning done, grocery shop, go to the hairdresser, do all of the things that she'd been neglecting due to her depression. As she mopped the kitchen floor her phone rang. She turned down the radio before answering.

"Hello."

"Brianna it's me. I still need four thousand more dollars. How much you got?"

Brianna was surprised and glad to hear Shan's voice. "I've been calling to tell you that I have seven thousand for you. I wrote you a letter. Have you open—"

Shan abruptly cut her off. "I'm on my way to come get it." *Click.* All Brianna heard was a dial tone. Still, excited that Shan was coming over, she hurried and finished with the kitchen. She showered and threw on the Prada jeans and blouse that Shan had bought for her. She was dying to talk to a female, especially her number one girl, since she had been living like a recluse ever since her and Shan fell out.

An hour and a half later she heard a knock at the door. "I'm coming Shan." The tears were rolling down her cheeks. "I miss you so much!" She swung the door open.

"We miss you too." This big black burly brother damn near knocked her backwards as he pushed the door open. He was followed by what looked like albino twins.

"Damn she fine," one of the twins said.

"Who the fuck are y'all?"

"Don't worry about who we are. You need to be worrying about what we're getting ready to do to your scandalous ass."

Brianna took off running towards her bedroom. The twin who said that she was fine ran behind her and snatched her up by her hair. Brianna began kicking, screaming, and scratching whomever she could get her hands on. The big black burly brother stuffed a handkerchief into her mouth and then began ripping off her clothes. She was still swinging and kicking like a wild animal. *Pop!* He punched her in the face.

"Hold this bitch down niggas!" Big black burly ordered. "Naw. Hold up. Maybe we should put her on the couch. She could take two of us at the same time."

"Fuck that! Take that rag outta her mouth. She could suck my dick and take all three of us!"

The other twin and big black burly laughed.

"Let's do it!"

They carried her back into the living room kicking and screaming with the gag in her mouth. Big black burly hurled her onto the couch.

The shorter albino twin was the first to drop his pants. Brianna's eyes got big as saucers and she was screaming and shaking her head no. Short albino's dick was so big that it definitely could have been his third leg. He sat on the couch and began giving orders as if they did this before.

"Get this bitch up and have her straddle me. While I'm beating up the pussy one of y'all could be tappin' that ass hole."

"That ain't gonna work man. Let's put her back in the bed. That way she could lay on top of you and I'll get on top of that ass. Or we can sixty-nine this hoe. I do know this couch ain't gonna work." Big burly snatched her back up and they went back into the bedroom.

Oh, God. Please, Shan, hurry up over. Brianna was praying to herself. *Please God, send her through that door right now.*

Little did she know that last night Shan had called Briggen over and told him that she needed a favor. He thought it was money. So as soon as he got to her house he asked her how much did she need. She told him that she didn't need money she needed a huge favor and that it was very important to her. After she told him what she needed Briggen asked her if she was sure. She looked crazed and bugged out; and assured him that she was very sure. So luckily the three dudes who were at Brianna's now were in town for a couple of days and were the type of niggas who would do anything. So Briggen put them on it in exchange of her promise to leave Forever alone.

They finally got Brianna in a position where one twin could hit the pussy and the short albino with the third leg decided he wanted to bust her a new ass hole. Brianna was in so much pain from being fucked in two holes at the same time she had fainted. But that didn't stop big black burly from throwing them legs up over his shoulders and continuing to beat that pussy up. After they were all satisfied they tied up her wrists and ankles and big black burly went to the kitchen and raided the fridge. They brung her back into the living room.

The twins sat down on the couch. Third leg grabbed the remote and began flicking channels. "Shut that noise up, bitch!" he yelled at her.

"Please go," Brianna pleaded. "Leave me alone," she screamed.

"Bitch I gotta hit that one more time," the taller twin said.

Big burly came into the living room carrying a bag of Doritos and was chomping on a turkey and cheese sandwich. "Damn. That hoe got some good pussy. You gotta man baby?" he joked, causing them all to burst out laughing.

The more the taller twin looked at her naked the hornier he got. "Fuck it!" He got up, scooped Brianna up off the floor and headed for her bedroom.

"Yo, what you doin' man?" Third leg's eyes followed his twin who ignored him. They heard the door slam. Minutes later they heard Brianna's gut wrenching scream and tall twin slapping her, telling her to shut up.

"Damn. Your brother into that S and M?" Big black burly forced a mouthful of Doritos in his mouth.

"I wouldn't call it S and M. But he do like to beat bitches up while he fuckin' them. He get off on that sick shit." He turned down the volume on the TV and they heard him beating Brianna. She was screaming "Oh, God, somebody stop him!" "See what I mean?" third leg said. Big black burly shrugged his shoulders.

Fifteen minutes later the door came open. "Yo come back here!" he yelled.

After the other two raped her again they stood up over her and pissed all over her body.

When Brianna finally woke up her whole body was aching, her head was pounding and she was lying in puddles of blood and piss. She snatched the handkerchief out of her mouth and her throat was so dry she began to gag. As her eyes focused the room began to spin. Then her body began to tremble as she cried herself to sleep.

When she awoke again it was pitch black outside. She remembered that she was supposed to go grocery shopping, get her hair done and drop by the cleaners. Her thoughts then went to her cleaning up, Shan calling, and as she waited for her to come over that's when that knock came and she was greeted with her worst nightmare. *What happened to Shan? Where is Shan?*

"Ahggg!" She groaned as her body peeled from the soiled sheets. She turned on her bedroom light and looked into the mirror. The left side of her face was swole, the right side was blue and black, her hair was matted to her neck and scalp. Her loose tooth was now gone. She looked as if she was auditioning for a horror movie. The stench in the room was horrendous. Her body was so sore that it took her almost twenty minutes to take the linen off the bed and throw it into a trash bag. She then thought about Shadee and Shan. She called them both only to get their voice mail.

She then dragged herself into the bathroom and turned on the shower. It was so hot her skin was turning red but she didn't care. She began crying and scrubbing her skin so hard she thought that her skin would begin bleeding. When she couldn't take the pain anymore she got out and dried off. When she sat down to pee it burned so bad she cringed in pain. That's when she decided to dial 911.

After being questioned by the police she was taken by ambulance to the hospital, the Med. She was assigned a rape crisis counselor and then given a thorough exam. She needed six stitches in her anus and she had a yeast infection. Two days later, before she was released, the doctor, with his back to her, told her that she was HIV positive.

"What?" she asked in disbelief.

He turned around, faced her and said again, "You're HIV positive."

"Doctor, please. Don't do this to me." She got up and went over and grabbed him. "Are you sure?"

"Yes ma'am. Here are your test results." He held up the folder.

"Noooo!" Brianna screamed. "That can't be right. You have to do them again! Doctor please," she begged.

"We can run the tests again but more than likely the results will be the same!"

"You don't know that!" Brianna screamed. "You don't know that!" She began trashing the room. Two nurses came running, along with a male nurse's aide to see what was all the commotion.

The nurse's aide grabbed her, held her, trying to soothe her. "You can get through this baby girl. C'mon now."

"Oh, Goddd!" She sobbed into his chest.

The Filipino doctor felt relieved because he was so scared that she was gonna attack him he thought he was gonna piss in his pants. "Nurse Richie, here are her discharge papers."

"Okay. I can handle it from here."

"Thank you." He then bolted for the door.

"Dr. Huron," Brianna yelled.

He reluctantly came back in. "Yes?"

"I was just raped less than seventy-two hours ago. Isn't it impossible to show up this fast?"

"Staff, please excuse me and my patient." When they all dispersed he motioned her to the chair. "Have a seat." He then handed her some tissue and waited until she finished blowing her nose. "To answer your question, yes it is impossible to show up that quick. That's why we had you list your previous sex partners. It had to be contracted from one of them."

As Brianna rode in the back of the cab her thoughts kept going back to Shadee. As she looked at the engagement ring on her finger she said, "He wouldn't do this to me! No. I know he wouldn't. That fuckin' nigga." Brianna kicked the back of the seat. "That nigga fucked me on purpose." *Calm down, girl.* She told herself. *You jumping to conclusions.*

"That'll be $14.40, ma'am." The cab driver interrupted her thoughts as he pulled in front of her apartment.

She gave him $15.00 and stepped out of the taxi like a zombie. All she saw was revenge. The closer she got to her front door the angrier she got. She couldn't open the front door because the tears wasn't allowing her to see. "Shit!" She kicked at the door, then wiped her eyes. "I hate y'all motherfuckers!" she screamed, finally getting inside where she immediately began trashing the place. "Who raped me goddammit!" she screamed. "Who infected me!" She was going berserk, tearing down the curtains, turning over the coffee table, throwing CDs everywhere. "I hate you all!" She moved from the living room to the kitchen where she wreaked more havoc. Tossing dishes, including her expensive china. Slipping on a plastic spatula she fell onto her ass. Crying hysterically she banged her head repeatedly up against the cabinet.

"God why do you hate me so much?" she screamed over and over before blacking out.

23

SHAN

I feel like I'm losing my mind. I don't even think logically any-more. For example, last week I invited Briggen over to ask him to send somebody over to Brianna's to fuck her over, just like she fucked me and my brother over. He asked me if I needed some money and me and my dumb ass said no. I was so bent on getting some payback. Now I haven't been able to get in touch with him to tell him, hell, yeah. I need some loot.

Now here I am, sitting in front of the prison, my job waiting on a bitch to come see her husband. Crazy ain't it? I feel like I'm falling and can't get up.

As soon as Shan saw Nyla and their daughter get out of a mini-van she got out of her car and walked towards them.

"Come on Tameerah." Nyla grabbed her hand.

Shan caught up to them. Her stomach was doing flips. "Um, excuse me. Can I talk to you for a minute?"

"Who are you and what about?" Nyla looked Shan over in con-tempt.

"I'm the computer teacher. Your husband works for me." She had Nyla's full attention but she wasn't gonna let her know it.

"Tameerah go stand behind Ms. Jenkins and hold our spot in the line baby."

"Okay Mommee." She gladly takes off running.

Nyla stops and stands where she can keep an eye on Tameerah. "So, who are you again?" Still looking at her like she's shit while noticing how Shan looks like she's stressed the fuck out.

"My name is Shan. Forever works for me. I'm pregnant by him." She paused, waiting on Nyla's response. Nyla looks at her like she's crazy. "I'm keeping it despite the fact that he wants me to get an abortion."

This bitch has a lot of fuckin' nerve and balls, stopping me and telling me this bullshit. Nyla was about to snap when Tameerah yells, "Mommee, c'mon. It's our turn!"

"I'm coming baby." Thankful that the sound of her voice brought her back to reality. The here and now. She calmly said, "I don't know you. And it's very hard for me to believe that you're that hard up for a man that you have to get a job at a prison to get some dick. All this free dick out here. So you need to take the bullshit elsewhere cause I am not the one. And I suggest that if you're liking my husband, you better do it from afar. As a matter of fact, I suggest you get another job, and fast. Because like I said, I am not the one." She stormed off leaving Shan standing there looking dumb. But after she thought about it she turned around, snapping her fingers and said, "Excuse me." Shan was still standing in the same spot, mouth hanging open. "My husband did tell me that there was a hoe in here harassing him while y'all are supposed to be gettin' money. He said he explained to you that this is business and that he needed you to bring his dope in and if it called for a little dick, well, he had to do what he had to do. So I gave him that. But he said you caught feelings. And now you want to have his baby? Girlfriend, I suggest you let it go. You see this diamond tennis bracelet?"—she held out her wrist—"thank you. I just bought this last week. And what? You can't even get him to give you four fuckin' lousy dollars to get your brother out?" Shan's hand went up to her chest. "Yeah. I know all about you. Hoe you being used, like some shitty toilet paper. Since you've been riding my man's dick, I've been wiping my ass with thousands."

Mr. Forever? He got me fucked up! Here I am holding it down for this nigga and he's on the inside fucking bitches? Oh, hell no! Once I get all of the facts, it's gonna be on. I'm getting ready to show him my true colors, Nyla screamed to herself.

"Bitch, I'm wifey. So whatever feelings you got for my husband that's all you got is feelings. Forever is mines, always and forever."

24

FOREVER

"Dayum dawg. That's fucked up. That's really fucked up." Zeke sat up in his bed for emphasis.

"I know man." Forever finally told Zeke that Shan was pregnant and refused to get an abortion. Zeke was so damn dramatic, which was why he really didn't want to tell him.

"So when you gonna tell wifey? Today when she comes? You know you gotta tell her before that hoe tells her!" Zeke fired at him.

"I know man." Forever dragged.

"You sound like you ain't gonna tell her."

"I'ma tell her. But not right now." Just then Forever heard his name over the intercom calling him for a visit. He was glad because Zeke was about to start grillin' him.

"You need to tell her today and get the shit over with!" Zeke yelled at him as he walked away. Forever acted as if he didn't hear him, concluding that he couldn't fill Usher's shoes. No, not today.

"What's going on, Thompson?" A cool white guard named O'Neill asked him.

"Same ole, same ole. What's up wit' you?" Forever asked as he began taking off his clothes for the visit. *It's a damn shame, you gotta strip before you go on the visit and strip when you come off of one. Shit's stupid. If you gonna bring something in they can't stop the shit no way. Stupid muthafuckers!* Forever thought to himself.

"Trying to survive, that's all." O'Neill sighed.

"I hear you man. That's the name of the game—survival." Those were the only words exchanged as he was processed through.

"Daddee! Daddee!" Tameerah flew across the room. *She looks just like her mother. I can't wait to get home and spend some quality time with her.* Forever smiled to himself.

"Here's my baby." He picks her up and gives her a big kiss on each jaw. "I miss you."

"I miss you too!" she yells as she hugs him around his neck.

"Where's your momma? You mean you're that big that you drove down to see me all by yourself? I didn't know you could drive," he teases her.

That cracks her up. "I can't drive Daddee. You know I'm too little to drive. My mommee drove me up here in our new truck."

"Then where is she?"

"She's in the bathroom." She said it as if he was supposed to know that.

"Oh okay." She didn't give Forever a chance to steal another kiss because she started squirming, trying to get down.

"I want a strawberry ice cream, Daddee." She meant strawberry yogurt. Nyla had tricked Tameerah into thinking that yogurt is ice cream. She was now pulling Forever towards the vending machines.

"How'd you get so strong?" Forever teased her.

She stops and flexes her arm. "I got muscles like my friend Dayshawn. And last night I ate all of the vegetables on my plate."

"I see." Just then Nyla comes out of the bathroom. Forever stares at her with pride, thinking that she is soo fine. Her complexion is so smooth without a single blemish. She has on one of Forever's favorite "we are gonna fuck today" skirts and blouse. Ma Ma has always been down for whatever. He enjoys the scenery as she comes over to the vending machines.

"Mommee, give me the money for my ice cream please."

"Hey baby." Forever steals a kiss and rubs his hand over that nice ass. She tenses up. "You a'ight?" He slaps it to make it jiggle. She doesn't respond to him.

"Is there anything else you want outta here?" she asks Tameerah as she places the five dollar bill in the slot for the yogurt.

"Can I have a Nestle Crunch too?" Then she looks at Forever. "Daddee what do you want?"

"I want an ice cream like you."

"Mommee, Daddee wants ice cream too."

She gets two of them and gives them to Tameerah who runs to their table and sets them down. Then she dashes back and gets some napkins. "What's up?" He asks Nyla as he leans over to kiss her on the lips.

"You got something you want to tell me?" she fires at him.

"Where's my kiss? I miss you. I know Daddy can get a kiss." He teases her.

"I don't think so."

Now what the fuck is her problem? He's thinking to himself. *I know she don't know about Shan.* Guilt was already settling in. "What I do?"

"I'm waiting on you to tell me," she snaps back.

"What did Daddee do Mommee?" Tameerah asked.

"I'm waiting on Daddee to tell me."

"What'd you do Daddee?" She looks up at him with that face of innocence.

He shrugs his shoulders and pokes out his lips in a pout and Tameerah starts laughing. They both eat their yogurt as Nyla sits with her arms crossed, obviously pissed off.

As soon as Tameerah finishes off her yogurt she asks to go play with the toys. She runs off without giving Forever a kiss. *What's going on with the women in my life?*

"So Forever, do you have something to tell me?"

"What are you talking about Nyla?"

"Forever don't play with me. What are you holding from me?" The longer she stared at him the more paranoid he got.

"Nyla if you got something to say, come on wit' it."

"I don't have shit to say, not yet anyway. You are the one who has fucked up! Not me."

Aww shit! Beads of sweat were forming on his top lip and he could feel the moisture forming under his armpits. *I know she don't know. I just told Zeke on my way out here. That was a few minutes ago. Shan don't even know Nyla.*

"What? Cat got your tongue?" She was really beginning to fuck with his head. "I tell you what Mr. Forever. I'ma make a deal with you. I'm going to get me a cup of coffee and when I come back if you are not ready to tell me what you have to tell me, I'm walking outta here and you will never, ever see me or your daughter again. On the flip side, you tell me what's up and I just might work with you."

Before he could swallow the huge lump that had formed in his throat she got up and headed for the vending machines. He was sure that all of the color drained from his face because he was feeling quite peaked. He was busted but the big male ego and that fabulous male pride is a muthafucker! He couldn't admit that he was guilty of the ultimate fuck-up! He looked around the room because it was feeling like all eyes were on him but actually no one was paying him any attention. He was just paranoid as hell. The guilt wouldn't allow him to look at his wife as she headed towards him. It felt like the closer she got to him the more powerful her aura was. His mind was definitely playing tricks on him. After what seemed like forever, she finally sat down, still holding onto the cup of hot, steaming coffee. She sat there looking at him, refusing to break the silence. He couldn't look at her. His eyes were glued to that cup of hot, steaming coffee. He knew he wasn't about to confess to shit as long as she was holding onto that.

"Forever." After a few seconds she finally said something.

"What? If you got something to say Nyla, then say it," he said, trying to see what all she knows.

"This . . . is . . . my . . . last . . . time asking. Is there something you want to tell me?"

He got bold. "Nyla, what the fuck are you talking about?" Then he sees the coffee cup go up. He covered his face with his arms while biting down on his lip to keep from screaming. "Shit, Nyla!" he curses while tearing off his shirt. "Shit, Nyla! That's fucked up!" The majority of the skin areas that the coffee hit were already turning red. A couple of blisters were starting to form.

"Shit!" Only a few people noticed what had happened. Nyla was sitting there just as calm, arms and legs crossed, wearing a smirk on her face. "Why the fuck you do that Nyla? Damn! Look how red my arms are. That could have been my eyes Nyla. I know they are not going to let me go change shirts and come back."

"Come back? Nigga I already told you I'm outta here. I gave you a chance Forever. Several chances! So you know what? If that hoe means that much to you, y'all look good together. Fuck the both of y'all. Nigga take a long good look at your daughter, you worthless piece of shit! Tameerah, time to go baby," she yelled as she stood up.

"No baby. Wait." He began pleading like a bitch. "Please. Don't leave. It was just business. I was—" *Pop!* He was startled. Nyla, his baby, had just punched him in the mouth.

"Ha ha haa. Daddee. Mommee punched you." Tameerah was laughing at him as she ran over to where they were.

"Go back and play baby." Nyla told her. They watched her run back to the play area. "Nigga please! If it was just business then why is the hoe saying she pregnant Forever?" She reached over and slapped him again. He got up, because he needed a minute to get the balls to confess and needed to change his shirt. It had cooled off but his arms were stinging.

"Don't walk away from me. How could you do this to me? To us?" she seethed.

"Let me see if they will let me change shirts. Please wait for me. Don't leave baby, a'ight?"

She jumped up and went towards the bathroom.

* * *

After some serious negotiating, Forever was allowed to go wrap gauze around his blisters and put on a clean shirt. He eased by Zeke's cell and was praying and hoping that Nyla was still out there. It was time to face the music. At least, he was gonna try.

"You all right Thompson? I heard you had quite a mishap out there earlier. How did I miss it?" O'Neill questioned him.

"Wasn't nothing to miss. Don't be listening to fools around here. They just want something—anything—to talk about." Forever snapped while hoping this clown wasn't going to make him cuss his ass out. Now was not the time for jokes. He was relieved to see that Nyla waited for him. She was still pissed off and was holding their daughter who had dozed off.

"Do you love her?" She didn't give him a chance to sit down.

"Excuse me?"

Pop! She punched him once again in the mouth while holding Tameerah.

"Do you love her?"

"No Nyla. I love you and only you. And she's lying about being pregnant. I'm sorry Nyla. I had the opportunity, and I took advantage of it. I fucked her but I know she ain't pregnant. It was very irresponsible of me and I'm sorry. I fucked up."

"You damned right you fucked up! You don't know what that bitch got! And look at you. You still lying! One thing for sure, two for certain, you betta get that bitch to get rid of it because I know she's pregnant Forever. Do you understand me?" He nodded his head yes. "Answer me!" she yelled as if he was a child in serious trouble.

"I understand Nyla, damn," he conceded. He was cold-busted.

"Now as far as I'm concerned the bitch is expendable. Am I right?"

Damn. My baby is cold-blooded. She shocked the shit out of him. He immediately knew what she was getting at.

"Am I right?" She snapped.

"Yeah baby. You know the bitch is expendable. I was just using her to get that money. You know we gotta eat."

"Well good. Because she is now your get outta jail free card. When is the next drop?"

"Damn Nyla, you gonna turn me into a snitch?"

"Nigga you just said the hoe was expendable. You ain't the one snitchin', I am. Now when is the next drop?" she snapped.

He got quiet because he had to mull this shit over in his mind. *I got less than two more years to do, or if Nyla has her way I'll be out in less than a year but I'll be labeled a snitch.*

"Forever, it's either me and your child or her."

"Baby you know what I say about snitching. It's gotta be something else we can do."

"Nigga I already told you what the deal is. And I'm not going to say it again. It's either me or her. You know what? Fuck it! If it was all about me, I wouldn't have to convince your ass! I promise you. This will be the last you ever see your daughter if you don't get your mind right and act like you know. You can think you're the HNIC if you want. But truth be told I'm runnin' shit. And don't you forget it! C'mon Tameerah."

He sat there dumbfounded as he watched his wife drag their child out of the visiting hall. "Fuck!" He leaned back and closed his eyes.

"Thompson! Let's go! You don't have a visitor out here," the lieutenant yelled at him.

I need to go to the hole because I swear if I see Shan, I'ma bust her in her ass. She didn't have to tell Nyla, scandalous bitch!

25

THE END

"How could I be so fucking stupid? This muthafuckin' nigga has been playing me from day one. I can't believe this shit!" Just the thought was making Shan gag. "The bitch even knew the amount of money I was begging the nigga for. How could I be so fucking dumb?" Shan had already decided that she wasn't shedding another tear. She got played big time. So what? It wasn't the first time and damn sure wouldn't be the last. Life goes on.

Even though Peanut had a house with Keke he kept an apartment on the side. He wanted Shan to go by and move out the valuable stuff and put it in storage. He didn't want to take chances and get his shit stolen.

"Peanut!" She sighed as she looked around the apartment. "How the fuck? You know what?" she said to the movers, "Take everything out!" I'm not sorting through all of this shit!"

"All right ma'am," the Mexican mover with Jose on his name tag responded.

"I don't know what's valuable to him or not and I don't want to hear his mouth. Take it all," she repeated.

Five and a half hours later everything was gone except for the dishes in the kitchen cabinet. As she began packing the top shelf, she came across a black cosmetic bag. "I know this nigga ain't got no dope in here," she snapped as she zipped it open. Her eyes almost popped outta their sockets as she ran her hands over the stacks of hundred dollar bills. "One, two, three, four, five, six, seven, eight, nine, ten, eleven, twelve, thirteen! Thirteen damn thousand dollars! I've been out here doin' Lord knows what to get money and this fool got money all along! That stupid muthafucker! All the trouble he got me into!" Shan was pissed off but at the same time happy that she could now get her brother out. She couldn't believe it.

After Brianna was raped and told that she was HIV positive she was devastated. She began chain smoking, having nightmares, breaking out in bouts of hives, becoming a nervous wreck. She kept thinking that someone was at the door, severe paranoia was creeping in. The idea of suicide was becoming more and more appealing to her. Shadee had went out of town again and was calling her, blowin' up her voice mail. She had to get her mind together before speaking with him. It has been almost two weeks since their engagement and her diagnosis. She was trying to figure out one: who were the men who raped her and two: if Shadee was infected and had purposely infected her.

She had to know for sure. If she could find out definite facts, payback would be priority and suicide would have to wait.

The next time the phone rang and his name popped up on the Caller ID she forced herself to answer.

"Hello."

"Damn B. Where you was at? I've been callin' and callin'! What the fuck was you doin'?"

"I was right here Sha."

"Then why you wasn't answering the phone?"

"I need to talk to you. When are you coming home?" Her heart beat rapidly.

"Home? Bitch my home ain't with you!"

That caught Brianna off-guard. She was stunned, thinking something was the matter with her hearing. "What did you say?"

"Everybody was telling me that you wasn't shit and that you can't turn a hoe into a housewife. I didn't listen. But when you set me up, that's when my eyes opened. Payback is a mutha! But you see B, what you ain't know was that I ain't the one! You set up the wrong nigga. Why I say that? Because my payback is slow and deadly. BeeaaTCH! You been fuckin' an HIV-positive nigga! Go get tested hoe!" He turned off his phone.

Brianna dropped to her knees gagging and throwing up all over the carpet. She couldn't believe that Shadee would purposely do that to her.

After several days of drinking and smoking crack, Brianna hyped herself up to do what she had to do. Nick was gone. So that plan was shot down. Shadee played her big-time. So did Peanut. Shan, her only real family, was history. So was Peanut. She had a locksmith open the safe that Shadee had at her apartment, emptied out the contents and went looking for Shadee. After the fourth day he showed up at his apartment with Doc and Teraney. After about an hour they all came out and got into separate cars. Brianna started up her car and followed Shadee to what she recognized as Janay's house. She watched him go inside. She sat in her Lexus suckin' on that glass dick, for about two hours. After it was all gone and she was so geeked up she jumped outta the car and banged on Janay's door.

When Janay opened the door Brianna pushed it open, damn near knocking Janay over, and ran over to Shadee. He was sitting on the couch wondering why Brianna was standing over him.

"What the fuck is your problem Brianna?" As soon as he stood up Brianna pulled out the burner that she took out of his safe. "How'd you get that girl?"

"Nigga I'm sending you to meet your maker." She aimed the burner at him.

"Not in my house bitch. Take y'all's beef outta here Shadee," screamed Janay.

"Shut up hoe!" she yelled, not taking her eyes off of Shadee. "I was going to make things right by you Shadee. I set you up but at least you are not dead. But you turn around and pull this shit! Play me like I'm some goddamned board game! You even had the nerve to propose to me?" Her hands were trembling as well as her voice.

"He did what!" Janay screamed. "You did what nigga?" She was now all up in his face. Disregarding the fact that Brianna was standing there with a gun.

"Janay baby, listen."

"Don't Janay baby me!" She started crying. "What have I ever done to you Shadee, but be a goddamned good ass woman and mother to our son?"

"Bitch move the fuck outta my way," Brianna warned.

Janay turned around looking like a madwoman. "You in my muthafuckin' house bitch. Let's not forget that. That gun you're holding does not scare me. If you was going to use the muthafucker you would have done so minutes ago." Then she turned back to Shadee.

"Baby I was only pla–"

"Shut the fuck up nigga!" She picked up her crystal vase and smashed him in the head. He screamed out. "Let me talk! I've been with your sorry, no good, homosexual ass for how long? Being faithful and you ask this gold diggin' bitch to marry you?"

"Baby fuck her. It wasn't even like that! Listen . . . I—"

She gave him the hand. "You know what? This is the last fuckin' straw! This is the straw that broke this goddamn camel's back! I was willing to work with your HIV infected, homosexual, faggot, wanna be a thug ass. I don't know what the fuck I was thinking. Thanks bitch, for snapping me outta my madness," she said to Brianna. "I'm outta here. Shoot that fuckin' punk! I'll send you the bill!" And she headed towards the door hoping that Brianna did kill his ass. That way her secret would go with him to his grave.

"Janay call the cops on this crazy bitch! She lyin!" he yelled after her.

She moved closer to him looking even crazier. "Oh, so I'm lying now?" *Pop!* She aimed at his dick but shot his thigh instead.

"Oh, shit girl! C'mon, Brianna." He tried lunging at her.

"Get your ass back nigga. Sit, doggie!"

"Brianna stop playing!" He was pressing his thigh in an attempt to stop the bleeding.

"Nigga I ain't playin'. I'm just wondering how I can make your ass suffer. *"Pop!"* She shot him in the other thigh, making sure he couldn't go anywhere.

"Oww! Brianna please. We can arrange something, I got money. How much you need?" he pleaded. "Aww fuck, this hurts Brianna."

"What good is money going to do now?" She picked up the phone. "I know what. Since you like getting fucked in the ass I got something for you. You remember Big Freddie right?"

He was looking at her trying to figure out who he was.

"Nigga don't look crazy. Freddie—the one with them big ass dogs. He be puttin' on them freak shows with them. Oh yeah. Them big ass dogs will love fuckin' you in the ass. Better yet, he can videotape you sucking the dogs' dicks and getting fucked in the ass. I could make mad loot off that shit." Brianna smirked as she dialed Freddie's number even though he was already on his way.

"Brianna hold up, wait a minute."

"Naw, it's too late for that, beaatch! Ain't that what you told me over the phone?"

"Hello."

"Brianna," he screamed. "I got some info about your girl Shan." This caught Brianna by surprise. "What did you say?"

"I got some info about your girl Shan."

"What kind of info?"

"Hang up the phone." When he saw her hesitating he yelled,

"Now B. Hang up the fuckin' phone. This is important." As soon as she hung it up he ordered, "Put the gun down."

"No Sha. I am not putting down my damn gun. Now you want the next bullet in your dick, or what? That's what's going to happen if you don't say what you got to say."

"You not gonna get the dogs over right?"

"Nigga what about Shan?"

"She dropping a package off at the prison tomorrow and it's a setup."

"Package? What kind of package?"

"What the fuck you think Brianna? Dope!"

Brianna couldn't believe her ears. *Her girl moving dope? Aw, hell, no! Not Miss Goody Two-Shoes.* "How do you know this, Sha?"

"What kind of question is that? You obviously don't know who I am."

Just then they heard dogs barking. Shadee panicked. "Brianna baby, come on. Don't do this. We go too far back." He was sniveling and groveling like a bitch, as she was grinning and backing up towards the door. She opened the door and in came two huge animals with Freddie and his boys, Gino and Wayne Wayne, right behind him. Gino was the cameraman and he was carrying the equipment. *Damn, I wonder if a dog can get infected.*

"Yo Freddie, don't listen to that bitch; she crazy man," Shadee was begging. He had seen the dogs in action before with crack hoes; so he knew they could fuck humans.

"Yo, Gino . . ."

Smack! "Shut up, nigga." She grabbed a handkerchief from Freddie and stuffed his mouth. "Set that shit up right here," she yelled over the barking dogs. I can't watch this shit. I'ma be in my car." She held out her hand and Freddie gave her three eight balls and she skipped out to her car. As far as he was concerned, big ballin' Shadee, on tape suckin' off a dog was worth far more than three eight balls.

* * *

Two hours later and geeked the fuck out, she heard barking and they were coming out. Freddie handed her another eight ball as a bonus and they got in their rides and left. When Brianna went into the living room she had to hold her nose. It looked and smelled like a disaster area.

Shadee was on the floor looking half dead. Blood and shit was all over his naked body and she kicked him to see if he was alive. He barely whispered, "Get me an ambulance."

"You don't need shit nigga, but a body bag!" *Boom! Boom! Boom!* She put three to his head. "I ain't touch shit but this phone." She used her blouse to clean it off and ran out to find Shan.

"Who is it?"

"It's me." Brianna's heart thumped as she anticipated her girl opening the door. "Please Shan. Open the door."

Shan was on the other side with one hand on the chain, the other on the doorknob and her forehead resting on the door. Feelings of anger, hatred, compassion and flashes of their years of being together were all fighting for her attention. Brianna was on the other side with her ear to the door. The tension was so thick you could cut it with a knife but they could both feel each other's presence.

Finally Shan cracked the door. "What do you want?" she asked, not looking at her used-to-be best friend.

Brianna was trying to get a look at Shan. "This is important. I can't say it out here. It's about your drop tomorrow."

"What?" Shan had to have heard her wrong.

"It's about your drop tomorrow."

Shan put her hand over her heart wondering how in the hell Brianna knew about her drop. She closed the door, took the chain off and held it open. When Brianna walked in Shan did a double take. "What the fuck happened to you?" she blurted out as she looked at her friend from head to toe in horror. Brianna just stood there frozen, tears running down her cheeks. Shan noticed that her hair was so dry-looking, it was lifeless and the ends were so raggedy. Her skin color was ashen, her eyes were swollen. Her nails were obviously being bitten and her front tooth was gone. She looked as if she hadn't had a bath in days and the sweats she had on were hanging off her ass.

"Brianna what happened to you?"

"I don't know Shan. I couldn't even begin to start explaining. It's not important. I'm just glad to see you. Glad to be here. I miss this place so much. I'm not the same no more Shan. Nothing's the same. Anyway I'm not important. Shadee said tomorrow when you go to make that drop, the po-po are gonna be waiting on you. I just wanted to warn you. It's the least I can do. And for whatever it's worth, I'm sorry." Brianna hurriedly left, leaving Shan standing there dumbfounded and looking as if she had just seen a ghost.

Brianna got in her car and drove home. She sat in front of her house talking out loud. "What's the use? I have nobody. I fucked up my life, Shan's, and Peanut's. Fuck dying slow." She put the gun to her head and blew her brains out.

Nyla was sitting on pins and needles as she watched every car pass her except for Shan's. She had used all of her connections to put this show on. She couldn't do this jail thing another day. She couldn't. The fact that this happened was both a blessing and a trial. She now knew the true meaning of watching what you pray for. She spent countless nights lying in her bed all alone wanting so bad for Forever to come walking through the door. She would end up masturbating, crying herself to sleep and awaking with a terrible headache. Her contact at the DA's office promised her that this drop would get her man home in a few months. She had been so excited that she had been planning for it every day. The downside was Forever fucking this hoe, unprotected, and now she was carrying her husband's seed. *Did he love her? Would she keep the baby? Would the bitch and the baby be in their lives for-*

ever? "Damn you Forever!" She banged on the steering wheel as she cried until she felt dizzy.

Here it was damn near seven hours later and Nyla had tears in her eyes as she headed back to her home. All she wanted more than anything else in the world was for her man to come home. She felt defeated and all of her effort was in vain. She had been parked several blocks down from the prison, anxiously waiting to see the look on Shan's face as she drove by in handcuffs.

But all she got after the longest wait of her life was a phone call. Her contact in the DA's office told her that Shan never showed up. She had called in and accepted an offer to work at the new FCI in Victorville, California.

As for Shan, the last pick up she did for Forever was just that; the last pick up. She turned that package over to her brother who had come home the night before. That was his *come-up*. They stayed up all night packing and saying good-bye. Peanut didn't want her to go but she had to get a new start.

Shan hugged her big brother for the last time. She jumped into her ride and headed off. If he knew of the stop that she was about to make he would kill her himself.

When she pulled up on Brianna's block, police were every-where; also an ambulance. She slowed down, rolled her window down and asked a young girl what was up.

"Yo, that chick who drives that pimped up Lex blew her brains out in it. Yo, that shit was just like on TV! She fucked that ride up! Blood, brains, and shit was everywhere!" the young girl said excitedly.

Shan rolled her window up. The bag that she had packed for Brianna she threw in the backseat. She took one last look at her town house and the Lex and headed for the West Coast.

She came to the conclusion that everyone had a hustle; that's why you can't knock nobody's.

PAYBACK IS A MUTHA

WAHIDA CLARK

ABOUT THIS GUIDE

The suggested questions are intended to enhance
your group's reading of this book.

DISCUSSION QUESTIONS

1. Do you know or have ever crossed paths with a chick like Brianna?

2. What things did Brianna do to give the impression that it was all about her?

3. Peanut's asking Brianna to make a run for him, was it justification enough for Brianna to retaliate by setting him up?

4. What was your response upon learning about Shadee's extracurricular/secret activities?

5. What are your thoughts on the letter that Brianna wrote to Shan?

6. To get Peanut out of jail did Shan go to the extreme?

7. Was Shan's payback for Brianna a little extreme?

8. What do you think about Briggen? Was his actions selfish when he found out Forever and Shan were kickin' it?

9. Was Brianna's punishment for all of the harm she caused too severe?

10. Does it seem that Forever got off scott-free? Should he pay for any of his actions?

11. What are your thoughts about Nyla's plan backfiring?

12. Were you surprised to see that Shan turned out to be just as scandalous as Brianna?